KID FURY

The remote settlement of War Smoke lies quiet — until the calm is shattered by a gunshot. Marshal Matt Fallen and his deputy Elmer spring into action to investigate. Then another shot rings out, and cowboy Billy Jackson's horse gallops into town, dragging its owner's corpse in the dust: one boot still caught in its stirrup, and one hand gripping a smoking gun. Meanwhile, the paths of hired killer Waco Walt Dando and gunfighter Kid Fury are set to converge on War Smoke . . .

MICHAEL D. GEORGE

KID FURY

Complete and Unabridged

LINFORD
Leicester

First published in Great Britain in 2014 by
Robert Hale Limited
London

First Linford Edition
published 2016
by arrangement with
Robert Hale Limited
London

A catalogue record for this book is available
from the British Library.

ISBN 978–1–4448–2681–4

Published by
F. A. Thorpe (Publishing)
Anstey, Leicestershire

Set by Words & Graphics Ltd.
Anstey, Leicestershire
Printed and bound in Great Britain by
T. J. International Ltd., Padstow, Cornwall

This book is printed on acid-free paper

Dedicated to my old pal Colin Wall

Prologue

The Red Dog was the only saloon in Cougar Bluff and, as the sun finally set, it became the busiest place in the sprawling town as the small grey pony was steered towards it. The sky was red and seemed to make every pane of glass along the main street appear to be alight. The young horseman was far younger and smaller than most men who rode the West but he was just as dangerous. He had learned to use his pair of .44s at a tender age. Not because he had wanted to become a gunfighter but because he knew it was the only way he might survive.

Jim Fury had been heading west for nearly half his eighteen years. Along the way he had been tagged with the nickname of Kid Fury.

It was a handle which had stuck.

As with all youngsters he wanted to

be taller and stronger than all of his contemporaries, but nature had had other ideas for the horseman. He had barely managed to grow over five feet in height and, with his boyish good looks, seemed doomed to retain the appearance of a perpetual child.

Yet Kid Fury was no child.

He had seen and done more in his brief existence than most men three times his age. He had become an expert rider and his daring on horseback had ensured he was always able to work on cattle drives and ranches. He could rope better than any cowboy and had a speed with his guns which had become almost legendary. Stories that he was also a hired gunslinger who did other men's killing for them were rife, yet only he knew the truth. Even though he was one of the fastest draws in the West Kid Fury had never hired out to anyone in order to kill. Even if he had not grown since he had reached his sixteenth birthday, the stories about him had.

It seemed that everyone had heard of him but no one ever seemed to believe that the small rider could possibly be the real Kid Fury, for the Kid was reputed to be one of the fastest gunmen alive.

Everywhere the Kid went he had to prove himself over and over again. It had become a wearisome fact of his brief life but one he was used to. He had realized as soon as he had entered the outskirts of Cougar Bluff that the odds were stacked pretty high that once more he would have to demonstrate his speed with his six-shooters.

The Kid turned the grey pony towards the Red Dog and approached the nearest trough and hitching rail. He eased back on his reins and stared around the street as the last rays of the day ebbed away. A hundred faces had watched his slow ride into the town and up to the saloon but not one had been impressed by the sight. Fury knew that most of the folks who had watched his arrival simply thought he was a young

3

farmer's son or the like.

Even his pair of matched .44s in the hand-tooled holster failed to impress any of them. Many youngsters wore guns but it did not mean they knew how to use them. Most of those his age tended only to use their guns as hammers when repairing fences.

The Kid looped his right leg over the head of his mount and slid to the ground. He secured his reins around the twisted hitching rail and stepped up on to the boardwalk outside the noisy saloon. Even with the three-inch heels of his boots he was a tad shy of being able to see over the top of the swing doors. The windows were covered in the standard painted decoration that all saloons boasted, so, apart from the level of the noise coming from within the building, Kid Fury had no indication of what to expect when he entered.

He checked his holstered Colts and flicked the small safety loops off their hammers. It had become more than a habit. It had often become a survival instinct. He had walked into many a drinking hole only to be greeted by a hail of gunfire. Not all badmen were locked up behind bars. In fact the majority of them still roamed free and never gave a second thought to killing anyone who made the mistake of getting in their way.

Fury had learned long ago that every saloon in every town appeared to have someone within its four walls who could not control themselves and would turn on anyone they considered unable to defend themselves. His size was like a magnet to that breed. A lot of well-liquored large men could not resist picking on anyone smaller than themselves.

Maybe it was the rotgut liquor, or maybe it was because some men were just plain evil. They could never stop at simply taunting those they thought were unable to fight back. They would keep pushing and pushing, and then there were a few who would become insanely violent with either their fists or their guns.

The Kid knew that simply being different was a threat to a lot of people.

Fury pulled his Stetson down over his brow, stared from under its brim and pushed the swing doors apart. He entered the smoke-filled saloon and kept his eyes focused on the long bar counter straight ahead of him. The Red Dog was full to overflowing with men of various types and ages. Some were playing keno, whilst most played poker. The most dangerous were those who simply drank far too much whiskey and fuelled their aggression. A few bargirls of dubious age wandered around the saloon in search of clients as Kid Fury continued across the sawdust-covered boards until he reached the bar.

The youngster knew he had drawn the attention of all of the saloon's patrons. He could feel their eyes burning into him like branding-irons.

The bartender struck a match and lit the wick of a lamp on the bar. He lowered the glass funnel and turned the brass wheel. Light spread along the wet top of the counter until it reached the Kid. The flickering gleam made the Kid appear even younger than he really was.

The bartender walked to the Kid, leaned one hand on the counter and looked at him curiously.

'What ya want?'

Before the Kid could answer, a gruff, mocking voice came from a table behind him. Five men had been sharing a bottle of rye; now one of them, ignoring his companions, rose to his feet. He was big and most of his belly hung over his gunbelt buckle.

'Give the little boy a soda pop, Charlie,' he mocked.

Kid Fury did not turn. He stared into the mirror behind the bartender and watched the reflection as the large man moved towards him.

'Beer,' Fury said in a low whisper.

The bartender nodded. 'Beer it is.'

The large man raised his voice even louder. 'I said soda pop, Charlie. Don't go giving a man's drink to a little baby.'

Laughter came from all sides as Kid

Fury remained with his back to the speaker. He continued to watch the large figure's every move.

The bartender started to fill a glass with beer. 'Go sit down, Frank. We don't want trouble. The sheriff is on his rounds about this time and he ain't got a sense of humour.'

The large man reached the Kid. He rested against the bar counter and looked down at the youngster.

'You sure are dressed pretty,' the man named Frank mocked. 'Did your ma dress you, boy? Does she know you're here?'

Fury did not respond. He had heard every insult there was over the years that he had ridden alone in the West. He knew that the best bet was never to respond unless there was no choice.

The bartender placed the glass of beer down and accepted the silver dollar. 'I'll get ya change.'

Kid Fury nodded.

'Are you deaf, sonny?' Frank asked.

'Leave him alone, Frank,' one of the

8

men at the table said. He filled his glass with whiskey. 'Ain't right to pick on critters half ya size.'

'I don't like children coming into saloons.' The large man snatched the beer glass and raised it to his mouth. He spat into the suds, then placed it back down. 'Drink it.'

Kid Fury did not look at the man. He continued to stare into the mirror.

'You drink it,' he said in a low, chilling voice.

Frank Drew seemed to grow even taller. 'What did you say to me, worm?'

'I said for you to drink it,' Fury repeated. 'It's got your spittle in it, so you drink it.'

'Why, you little runt.' The man grabbed the Kid's shoulder and then felt the gun barrel poke into his fat belly. He released his grip and stared down at the .44.

Kid Fury turned and tilted his head back. He stared hard up into the face of the aggressive man. 'I said for you to drink it. Now drink it or I'll blow a hole through your belly.'

The swing doors of the saloon parted and a skinny figure with a white moustache stepped in. The tin star gleamed in the coal-tar lamplight.

'Put that gun back in its holster,' the sheriff demanded. 'We got laws in this town and I enforce them. Nobody's allowed to shoot dumb critters even if they are a pain in the neck.'

'Thanks, Sheriff.' Frank Drew smiled as he watched Fury slide his gun back into its holster. He stepped back and looked the Kid up and down. 'What's a little boy like you doing with two guns in a fancy shooting rig?'

Fury accepted a fresh glass of beer from the bartender and downed it. He turned away from the counter and the mocking man, then walked towards the sheriff.

The lawman stopped him with a hand against his chest.

'Who are ya?' the sheriff asked.

The Kid looked at the sheriff, then glanced back at the large figure who did not know when to quit.

'My name's Jim Fury.'

'Kid Fury?' the sheriff queried.

Every eye returned to the Kid when they heard the sheriff mention the name they had all heard of. Frank Drew started to walk after the youngster.

The Kid nodded to the lawman. 'Yep. That's what they call me, Sheriff.'

'What ya doing in Cougar Bluff?' the sheriff asked. 'We don't cotton to gunfighters in this town.'

'I ain't a gunfighter, Sheriff.'

'Yes he is,' Drew bellowed out as his drunken hands adjusted his own gunbelt. 'You seen him pull a gun on me. He would have blown me apart if you hadn't have come in, Sheriff.'

'I came in for a beer,' Fury said. 'Nothing else.'

'Throw him into jail.' Drew curled his fingers around his own holstered gun. 'I bet he's wanted. Lock his little butt up.'

The lawman looked at Drew. 'Sit

down, Frank. Ya drunk.'

Kid Fury turned. He had started towards the swing doors again when Drew pulled his gun from its holster and cocked its hammer. Everyone inside the Red Dog scattered.

'Out of the way, Sheriff. I'm killing the gunslinger.'

The lawman made as though to move towards the snarling Drew when a white-hot blast erupted from the gun barrel. The deafening sound of the shot echoed around the saloon as the sheriff was hit in his chest and went cart-wheeling over a table. As the lawman crashed to the floor Kid Fury swung on his heels, hauled one of his guns from its holster and fanned its hammer just as a second shot blasted from Drew's six-shooter.

A chunk was blasted from the wooden wall beside the Kid but his shot had been more accurate. Fury saw the large man stagger backwards and topple into tables and chairs behind him. Frank Drew went to cock his hammer again, then he realized that his gun had already fallen from his hand because Fury's bullet had shot half his wrist away from his arm. What was left of the hand hung by a bloody sliver of flesh. Blood poured from the hideous wound.

'You shot my hand off, ya little bastard,' Drew yelled.

The Kid moved to the lawman and stared down at the dead face. He then glanced at the onlookers.

'Remember who killed the sheriff,' Fury said, pointing his gun at the snorting Drew. 'That varmint did.'

Frank Drew was growling like a wounded bear as he went to pick up his blood-covered gun from the sawdust with his left hand. 'I'm really gonna kill you now, Kid.'

The Kid looked up at the ceiling from where a wooden chandelier was suspended by a rope from the rafters. A dozen candles were burning inside glass globes around its circumference. The Kid aimed and fanned his hammer at it. He watched as his bullet severed the

13

rope. The large chandelier came crashing down heavily on top of the ranting Drew. The impact knocked him senseless.

All eyes were on the Kid as he rose up with the smoking Colt in his hand. Every man was stunned and speechless. None of them had ever seen such a display of marksmanship before.

'I'd lock that critter up before he wakes,' Fury said. 'I reckon that even here shooting a lawman is a hanging offence.'

The words had only just left the lips of the Kid when a score of men pounced on the unconscious Drew. The youngster backed away from them and holstered his gun.

Kid Fury pushed his way out into the now dark street. He stepped down to the sand, grabbed his reins, tugged them free of the hitching pole and threw himself up on to his saddle.

He spurred.

1

The bright moon cast its eerie light down on the winding trail as the young Bar Q cowboy rode towards the distant settlement at breakneck speed. Only the high canopies of the trees prevented the moon from making the well-trodden trail between the Bar Q ranch and the town of War Smoke appear as if it were the middle of the day and not the start of another long night.

Billy Jackson balanced high in his stirrups and urged his mount onwards. He had a thirst and knew where he could find a place to quench it. Far ahead he could see the lights of the distant town glowing like a thousand fireflies.

It was a lure no thirsty cowboy could ever resist.

As the powerful cutting horse galloped down from the tree line towards a series of massive rounded boulders another horseman moved his mount through the shadows between the rocks and watched the approaching cowboy. The eyes of the onlooker remained fixed upon the cowboy as his thin right hand reached down and pulled the long-barrelled Winchester from its saddle scabbard.

Cradling the rifle in his deadly grip the watchful horseman pushed the hand guard down and expelled a spent casing from the carbine's magazine. He eased the guard back up, curled a finger around the rifle's trigger and raised the weapon up. The wooden stock fitted the shoulder of its owner like a well-worn glove.

He stared along the barrel through the rifle sights at Billy Jackson as the cowboy rode nearer and nearer to him.

There was no hint of emotion in the expressionless features of the rifleman. Killing was something at which he had become expert. His finger stroked the rifle's trigger as the cowboy emerged from a cloud of trail dust and rode towards a gap between the big boulders.

It took one squeeze of the trigger to send the small ball of lead flying from the weapon's barrel. A plume of gunsmoke cut through the shadows and hit the young cowboy. Billy Jackson suddenly arched in agony. The cowboy felt himself being punched back by the sheer force of the bullet hitting him.

Balanced precariously as he was in his stirrups it did not take much to knock the cowboy off the back of his mount. A fountain of blood sparkled like a ruby necklace in the moonlight as the youngster toppled from his high perch. The noise of the rifle shot filled the ears of the horse as it continued to thunder on towards the distant town.

Billy Jackson fell helplessly to the ground. As he hit the unforgiving soil the cowboy bounced and then suddenly realized that his boot was trapped in the leather stirrup. It was one of the greatest fears of all cowboys. They were all used to falling from their mounts at some time but to have a boot trapped by its spur in a stirrup meant only one thing. It meant they were doomed.

The sound of the deafening shot was still echoing around the trees and rocks as the rifleman slid his Winchester back into its scabbard and turned his horse away from the gruesome sight he had just created.

Billy Jackson's terrified horse kept on galloping down towards the lights of the distant town. The shattering of bones sounded along the trail as the wounded cowboy bounced from one immovable obstacle to another. It was as if he collided with each tree and boulder as his mount desperately tried to flee from the sound of its master's pitiful cries.

The ruthless assassin watched until the cowboy had been dragged out of sight. The cloud of moonlit dust lingered above the blood-splattered ground as the lethal horseman dragged his reins to his right and rode back into the trees.

There would be many more shots fired before the arrival of a new day. The horseman steered his mount towards War Smoke and more unsuspecting victims.

*   *   *

The lantern-lit streets of War Smoke were busy, as they always were with the coming of nightfall. The sprawling settlement was full of men looking for something to spend their hard-earned money on. They had never had to look very far to find their own favoured brand of entertainment. There were as many gambling halls and saloons in the large town as could be found in Tombstone or Virginia City. Prosperous cattle ranches and several gold mines ensured there was always a regular supply of hard cash and men to spend it.

War Smoke served its purpose and fulfilled the needs of its varied population. For most of the year it was as quiet as many of its eastern counterparts, but every now and then the tinderbox ignited. Miners and cowboys had a way of riling one another in a way that few men in other occupations could ever do.

This was a settlement on the edge of mountain ranges that were filled with gold. Precious nuggets and golden dust had always been the root of trouble wherever they were discovered. The lust for gold was like a fever that infected the majority of the community and had the ability to poison even the purest of souls. Those who had the dust and nuggets often found to their cost that it made them nothing more than targets.

Those who did not have the precious ore were often drawn to those who did. Many of them devised ways of getting their hands upon it.

Most of those ways were deadly.

The bargirls knew how to use their assets to fleece their patrons for services rendered. The gamblers knew of other ways to strip men of their wealth either honestly or dishonestly, while the cowboys simply tended to envy the fact that miners always had more money to squander than they could ever earn punching steers.

There were so many gambling halls and so many games of chance that prospectors were often tempted to turn their small fortunes into far larger ones. A crooked roulette wheel here and a marked deck of cards there should have taught the victims a valuable lesson, but it seemed that some men never learned.

Night after night they would return to be swindled.

Then there were the transient card-sharps who visited War Smoke briefly but never left town without making a handsome profit. There were those who did not have the charms of the buxom bargirls or the skill of the gamblers but still wanted to get their hands on the gold that they knew filled so many hard-working men's pockets.

These men looked the same as the honest people who drifted into the remote settlement, but they were far from being cut from the same cloth.

In all societies there are those who

kill without a second thought, who have no understanding of guilt and do as they wish until they are stopped. Killers never look like killers and that is why towns like War Smoke have always needed men like Marshal Matt Fallen.

Men like Fallen could never be corrupted, for they never desired other men's fortunes. Matt Fallen walked tall and spoke in hushed tones. He was the law and he made sure that he did his best to protect those who were unable to protect themselves.

He had never flinched from his duty.

Fallen had never shied away from a gunfight if that was what it took to set things right. Yet, despite a reputation that was known throughout the territory, there were still those who dared to arrive in the sprawling town to try their luck.

They were not the type to gamble with the quicksilver card dealers. The murderous breed who believed they could have whatever they wanted, and get it by killing anyone who already possessed it, had no intention of playing cards. There were a lot of ways to kill and some men knew every one of them.

Marshal Matt Fallen could not stop them entering his town. All he could do was try to stop them doing their worst once they had arrived. Even if it meant risking his own life as he had done on countless occasions, the six-and-a-half-foot-tall lawman would always try.

That was his duty.

He was paid to protect and he earned his salary.

In all the years during which Fallen had worn the tin star on his vest he had never once been outdrawn in a showdown. The only bullets ever to hit his broad-shouldered frame had come from those who used the shadows to shoot from.

The cowards who liked to bushwhack the brave were found in every town in the West and the marshal had grown used to the constant threat.

Yet Fallen remained unafraid and

even more determined.

The marshal had been doing his regular rounds along the streets of War Smoke for nearly an hour since sundown. He had been checking that all the locked-up stores were safe from those who liked to get their provisions without paying for them.

He strode down the alley from the livery stable back towards Front Street when he caught the familiar aroma of his deputy's coffee drifting on the air. His office was directly across the street and its lamplight beamed towards Fallen's tall figure as he stepped on to the boardwalk. His experienced eyes darted from under his hat brim in both directions.

Experience had taught Fallen to sense when there was trouble brewing, but he had not suspected a thing as he walked across the sandy street, riders and vehicles passing him in both directions.

The door of the office opened wide to reveal his deputy standing with the coffee pot in his hand. Deputy Elmer Hook beamed as though he had just managed to lure his superior back to the office with his own special recipe for the perfect pot of coffee.

'Elmer.' Fallen paused in the door-way as his eyes noticed the familiar figure of the petite Angie Parker walking barefoot towards him. It was hard to tell how old she actually was but Fallen knew she must be at least seventeen. Poverty had a way of stunting the growth of a lot of people. Many never even survived as long as she had, yet no matter what her hard existence had thrown at her it had not taken away her natural beauty.

The tall marshal sighed at the sight of the beautiful female. She was the daughter of Ben Parker, the drunken owner of a small, ramshackle hotel at the far end of town. Fallen looked at her and the rags she wore and had been wearing for several years. A flimsy, moth-eaten shawl draped her tiny shoulders. She was cold and that angered the tall marshal. He knew that several charitable people in War Smoke had given her their cast-offs over the years but they had never found their way on to her tiny frame. Whiskey-sodden Ben Parker did not permit little Angie ever to look like anything other than a waif.

Unlike her father, Angie was polite and charming. She smiled constantly and that was why she was never without bruises.

Fallen noticed the bottle of rotgut whiskey in a wicker basket draped over her thin arm. He removed his hat and gave a respectful nod to the approaching female.

'Angie,' the marshal greeted her. 'Kinda cold for ya to be out, ain't it?'

'Pa needed some whiskey.' Angie smiled with a shrug.

The marshal had a thought. 'Hey, I've got an old coat in the office that I don't need. Would ya like to have it? It ain't much to look at but will keep the frost off them pretty little shoulders of yours.'

She shook her head as if frightened. Her long hair floated in the chilly air.

'Pa wouldn't allow that. He might get notions and whip me again, Marshal Fallen. I thank ya for the kindness, though.'

'If there's anything ya need just come here,' Matt Fallen said with a firm nod of his head. 'If Ben hurts ya, come and tell me. Right?'

Angie smiled and started on down the street through the crowds of men and heavily painted women who lingered. He knew she would never betray the brutal father who seemed to take pleasure in hurting her.

Fallen gave out a long, regretful sigh as he watched her disappear from view.

Elmer stepped forward. 'She sure is pretty.'

'That's the problem, Elmer,' the marshal replied. 'Seems like the prettier she gets the more her drunken father beats her. He won't be happy until she's six feet under.'

The deputy nodded in agreement.

'Ben blames Angie for her ma running out with that card-sharp all them years back. That poor child is nothing but a pitiful whipping-dog to Ben. He sure is a mean *hombre* and no mistake. Somebody ought to bring him down a peg.'

'Maybe somebody will.'

'I surely hope so, Marshal Fallen.'

A cold shiver traced the spine of the lawman as he turned and concentrated on the pungent coffee pot in his deputy's hands. 'What ya got there, Elmer?'

'I knew ya would be drawn back here when ya caught a noseful of my coffee, Marshal Fallen.' Elmer rushed back to the tin cups on the marshal's desk and started to fill them. 'I know that ya will just love it. Nobody can make coffee like me.'

Fallen hung his hat on the top of the stand beside the stove. He closed the office door.

'Yep. Nobody makes coffee that tastes anything like yours, Elmer.' Fallen rolled his eyes and inhaled deeply.

'How were ya rounds, Marshal Fallen?' Elmer filled the tin cup and handed it to Fallen just before the marshal sat down. 'I hope ya didn't go accepting no free cups of coffee from all the cafés ya walked past. I'd surely hate for ya delicate taste buds to be ruined before ya try my special brew.'

'I ain't had a drop of anything to drink.' Fallen ran his fingers through his dark hair. 'It's real peaceful out there, Elmer. Quiet. It's still early, though. I figure it'll get a tad noisier when everyone is all liquored up.'

Elmer stood watching Fallen with a smile which seemed to stretch across his face from ear to ear. Fallen glanced up.

'What ya want?' the marshal asked.

'I want ya to try my coffee, Marshal Fallen.'

'Why?'

'I tried me a different recipe.' Elmer winked. 'It tastes better than anything ya ever tasted before.'

'Hell.' Fallen sighed anxiously and

asked, 'What did ya do to make it different this time, Elmer?'

'Eggshells, Marshal Fallen.' The deputy grinned. 'Not just any old eggshells, mind you. Them's brown-coloured eggshells. I reckon it gives it body.'

'I got me an idea why they're brown, Elmer.' Fallen sniffed at the cup. 'There's something else in this concoction that I can't quite work out. What else did ya put in it?'

Elmer nodded excitedly. 'That'll be the gunpowder. Just a pinch to give it a kick.'

The marshal raised both eyebrows. 'Gunpowder?'

'That's right.'

Suddenly the unmistakable sound of a gunshot out in the street drew the attention of both lawmen.

2

Alerted by the sudden and unexpected noise of a gun being fired Fallen drew his own gun and ran across the office to the door. He swung it open and stepped out on to the lantern-lit boardwalk. His eyes studied everything illuminated by the street's lanterns. Every vehicle and every startled face.

Elmer was at his shoulder. 'Don't you go fretting none, Marshal Fallen. It could be just one of the Lazy D boys letting off steam.'

Fallen gritted his teeth. 'Maybe.'

The busy street was full of people who were now stationary as each of them looked down the street. The tall marshal stepped to the very edge of the boardwalk and grabbed the shoulder of one of the men closest to him. The man looked up at the towering figure and gave a slow nod.

'Any idea where that shot came from?' Fallen asked.

The man pointed. 'Somewhere down near the Golden Garter by my reckoning, Marshal.'

'Thanks.' Fallen looked at his unarmed deputy and shook his head. 'Get ya gun, Elmer. How many times have I gotta tell ya to keep that hogleg strapped on?'

The deputy ran into the office. He emerged with a scattergun in his hands instead of a pistol. He shrugged.

'I can't find my gun, Marshal. Will this do?'

Fallen rolled his eyes. 'It'll have to. C'mon.'

The lawmen forced their way through the crowd of men and women until they reached the large saloon. Everyone in the motionless crowd was staring at its brightly painted façade.

'I figure that fella back there was right, Marshal,' Elmer remarked. 'Every one of these folks is looking at the Golden Garter.'

The marshal looked at the crowd. 'Is

this where the shot came from?'

There was a united grunt.

'C'mon, Elmer.' Fallen cocked his hammer and marched into the large foyer of the most expensive drinking hole in War Smoke. Close in his shadow the deputy trailed with the hefty double-barrelled weapon clutched in his hands. Both men were ready for trouble should it raise its head. In all his days as the marshal of War Smoke Matt Fallen had never entered this particular saloon; he was surprised at what greeted his eyes. 'What kinda saloon is this, Elmer? It ain't like anything I ever seen before.'

'It caters for a certain taste, Marshal Fallen.' Elmer nodded knowingly and winked. 'Ya know the sort of critter I mean.'

The marshal stared at his deputy. 'Rich 'uns?'

Elmer placed his tongue in his cheek. 'Them too.'

Fallen made his way towards a white desk set against crimson drapes. He sniffed the air. The smell of gunsmoke filled his nostrils.

'Smell that, Elmer?' Fallen asked as they reached a desk counter that resembled something better suited to a hotel than a saloon.

Elmer nodded and narrowed his eyes. 'I surely do. Smells like my coffee.'

'Gunsmoke,' the marshal told him.

There seemed to be nobody in the large foyer. Fallen sniffed at the air and followed the scent of gunplay towards a handsome imported door with a brass shingle nailed to its surface.

'It says 'Private', Marshal Fallen,' Elmer said.

Fallen grabbed the handle with his free hand and turned it. The door was locked. He released his grip and went to raise his right boot.

'Reckon I'm gonna have to kick this pretty bit of lumber off its hinges, Elmer.'

'I wouldn't do that if I were you, Fallen.'

Both the marshal and deputy turned

to look behind them to see who had spoken to them. The sight of a man in a well-tailored white suit was unusual in War Smoke. Only the richest of the town's gamblers ever sported anything quite so garish.

'Dandy Jim Buckley,' Fallen said through gritted teeth. He walked across the highly polished floor towards the owner of the saloon. 'So you ain't dead in there? That'll disappoint a whole heap of folks.'

'What are you doing here?' Buckley asked in a voice which sounded as though it belonged on a riverboat. 'I didn't send for you.'

'There was a shot, Dandy Jim.' Fallen loomed over the gambler. 'And my nose tells me that that shot came from in there.'

Buckley raised an eyebrow. 'One of the customers simply got a little excited when he won a few thousand dollars with a pair of queens. He fired his gun. He was thrown out into the alley. I don't allow anyone to discharge their guns in the Golden Garter, Marshal.'

Fallen bit his lip, then forced a smile. 'I'd better not find a dead body out back of here, Dandy Jim. That might make me angry enough to arrest you.'

Elmer grinned. 'That white suit sure ain't the right colour to be wearing in one of our jail cells, Dandy Jim.'

The gambler was neither frightened nor intimidated.

'I'd not threaten me, Fallen. It's never a wise move. Some of my best friends pay your wages.'

'Kick the door down, Marshal Fallen,' Elmer urged.

Fallen raised an eyebrow and smiled. 'We'd best not do any damage in here, Elmer. Not until we have a damn good reason to do so, anyway.'

The deputy was disappointed. 'Ah, shucks.'

Buckley smugly placed a cigar between his teeth and struck a match with his thumbnail. 'Thanks for your concern.'

'C'mon, Elmer. The smell of perfume is kinda burning my eyes.' The marshal turned away from the gambler and marched back to the street with his deputy at his shoulder.

'Ya ain't gonna take his word are ya, Marshal Fallen?' Elmer asked as he dogged each step of the towering lawman. 'I reckon there might be a dead body in that office of his.'

Fallen pushed his way through the crowd and started back towards their office.

'Buckley is the kind of man who can rustle up trouble just for the sheer hell of it, Elmer,' Fallen said. 'I reckon it ain't worth the hassle of getting the town council on our backs again. Most of them are on his payroll. We just don't need that kinda bother.'

'What if I'm right, though?'

'We'll just have to keep our eyes peeled for any bodies that happen to crop up,' Fallen said. He stepped up on to a boardwalk and continued along towards the marshal's office.

The two men had no sooner reached their office when another deafening gunshot rang out at the opposite end of town. Fallen moved to the porch upright and rested a hand against it. Suddenly a saddle horse appeared from a side street and began to thunder in their direction.

'That's Billy Jackson's nag, Marshal Fallen,' Elmer pointed out.

The marshal's eyes narrowed as he focused on the limp body being dragged down Front Street by the wide-eyed horse. The lawman holstered his gun.

The seasoned marshal had no interest in the horse. All Fallen could see was the blood-covered body with one of its boots caught in a stirrup being dragged along as if it were a rag doll.

'And that's Billy,' the marshal said grimly.

Using his large frame to block the horse's advance, Fallen moved ahead of the thundering animal and started to wave his arms at it. The horse dug its hoofs into the sandy street and came to an abrupt halt a few feet away from the lawman. As he leaned forward and grabbed the reins of the terrified horse Elmer raced to where the bloody body lay in the sand, still clutching his smoking gun in his hand. The deputy released the cowboy's boot from the stirrup, then knelt down next to the horrific corpse.

'Mercy me!' Elmer grimaced. 'I ain't seen anyone this beat up before. Billy must have been dragged miles, but how come he fired his gun?'

'Either to try and stop the horse by killing it or just to try and get help. Reckon Billy was desperate when he fired his hogleg.' Fallen joined his deputy and knelt down. As both men carefully examined the body they heard the sound of Doc Weaver's instruments rattling in the aged medical man's battered black bag. The ancient sawbones' office was directly across the wide street where both lawmen knelt.

'What we got here?' Doc puffed as he reached the scene.

Fallen looked up at his old friend.

'Reckon this is a job for the undertaker, Doc. Billy is beyond your help.'

'Out of the way, Matt.' Doc carefully eased himself down on to one knee and started to check the body as Fallen rose up to his full height and rested his knuckles on his lips.

'I've not seen a cowboy bust up like that for many a while,' Fallen muttered. 'Only takes one mistake and even the best bronco buster ends up dead, I guess. Billy ran out of luck.'

Doc leaned back on his knees and looked straight up into the marshal's eyes. 'Bad luck didn't have anything to do with this, Matt.'

Fallen looked at his friend. 'What ya mean, Doc? He fell off his horse and got dragged, didn't he?'

Doc nodded. 'Yep, but he was shot first.'

'Shot?' The marshal crouched over the young Bar Q cowboy's remains and stared at the bullet hole hidden amid the blood and debris covering the cowboy. Doc Weaver had found it just under the tails of the cowboy's bandanna. 'Who in tarnation would shoot a poor cowboy? If somebody tried to rob him, he sure picked on the wrong breed of man. Cowboys usually ain't got enough money to last the night.'

'Not like gold miners,' Elmer added.

Doc Weaver accepted the help of both the lawmen to get back up on his feet. He stared down with sadness in his wrinkled eyes.

'Poor Billy. I recall bringing him into the world, Matt.'

'He was one of the quieter hands belonging to the Bar Q,' Matt Fallen said. 'He sure didn't deserve getting himself murdered.'

'Nobody does.' Doc sighed.

Elmer shook his head. 'Sometimes I plumb despair at the way folks kill one another for no reason, Doc.'

'Ya wrong, Elmer,' Marshal Fallen argued sadly with his deputy. 'There's usually a reason for folks to kill one another. Trouble is it ain't always easy to figure out what that damn reason is.'

41

Doc nodded. 'Ya right, Matt. Folks kill for a thousand reasons out here. Some are just petty 'uns but some got what they call 'motive' behind them. Gun law still rules most of the varmints out here in the West.'

Matt Fallen looked around the street. A thousand faces lit by the amber illumination of countless oil-tar lanterns and storefronts' lamps were watching the three figures, but most of the onlookers were only interested in staring at the dead cowboy. It was a morbid trait most men and women shared.

'Look at them, Doc,' Fallen said. 'Nothing draws a crowd like a dead man.'

'Naked gals can give them a run for their money,' Doc said. 'Yep, a naked gal gotta be real ugly not to draw a crowd.'

'Ya got a point there, Doc.'

Elmer shrugged. 'Shall I get a few boys rounded up to cart Billy off to the funeral parlour, Marshal Fallen?'

The elderly doctor raised a hand and

placed it against the deputy's chest. 'Get them to bring him to my office, Elmer. I'd like to check him over. There might be a clue on his young carcass to help us figure out who could have done this.'

'Doc's right,' Fallen said. 'Take Billy to his office and then get someone to ride to the Bar Q ranch and tell his pa what happened.'

Doc moved closer to the towering figure of the marshal.

'Bruno Jackson ain't gonna take the news well, Matt.'

'I know.'

'I sure hope he don't think you had anything to do with this,' Doc added. 'He did hire that gunslinger to kill you a while back, after all. Bruno might just reckon that this is revenge.'

'I'd never do anything like this.' Fallen glanced at the older man. 'Bruno and me have unfinished business but I ain't ever been able to prove nothing against him, Doc. His son is dead and I'll try to find out who did this. If

43

Bruno got half a brain he'll figure that out.'

Doc Weaver turned to go back to his office. 'The trouble is that Bruno ain't got half a brain, Matt,' he said as he walked away.

Elmer Hook looked troubled.

'Ya don't think Bruno will hire himself another gunslinger to try and kill ya coz someone's killed Billy, Marshal Fallen? Do ya?'

Matt Fallen ran a large hand across his neck. He did not answer. He did not know the answer.

3

The moon was high above the restless town. War Smoke had still not calmed down since the pitiful arrival of Billy Jackson. Few of the sprawling settlement's inhabitants had ever witnessed anything quite so horrendous before. Nearly every man, woman and child had seen death close up but the sight of the cowboy after he had been dragged into Front Street would remain with them until the day they too died.

It was obvious to the experienced Matt Fallen that Billy had been shot a long way from the centre of town, otherwise the fatal shot would have been heard by everyone in War Smoke. Neither Fallen nor anyone else had heard that shot.

Another thing troubled the lawman. Who had bushwhacked the young cowboy? And why? Why shoot someone who had little money on them?

Billy Jackson had no enemies, unlike his father. Maybe that was it, Fallen considered. What if some yellow belly had killed Billy for something Bruno Jackson had done?

Could that be it?

Matt Fallen and his deputy had left the body in the capable hands of Doc Weaver and made their way down to the nearest saloon. Both men were troubled but in different ways. For Fallen it was a matter of not knowing what his worst enemy, Bruno Jackson, might do when he discovered that his son Billy had been killed. The marshal expected that Jackson would again try to hire a gunslinger to destroy him. Fallen had never had any proof, but he knew that it had been Bruno who had paid for Texas Tom McCree to gun him down months earlier.

McCree had died in the attempt and taken the name of his employer with him, but Fallen knew only too well that being an honest and incorruptible lawman not only made him feared by wanted outlaws but also by those powerful people who lived in and around War Smoke. There were a lot of rich men in the town and they wanted to get even richer, but Fallen followed the law and had ruffled a lot of feathers.

Bruno Jackson had always managed to get his own way until the arrival of Matt Fallen. Since the appointment of the new marshal it had been a lot harder to get what you wanted by simply using gun law.

Even respected businessmen could find themselves standing on the gallows if the letter of the law was followed and vigorously applied. Fallen was dangerous and many wealthy men had paid to have him eliminated over the years. So far none of them had succeeded.

Elmer was also troubled, but for a very different reason.

The deputy had always been treated badly by the townspeople, apart from Doc Weaver. Not until he had been hired by Matt Fallen had anyone ever taken him seriously. If Fallen was killed it would mean the town returning back to its bad old ways and for Elmer Hook to become once again the brunt of others' jokes.

The deputy followed the marshal into the Silver Fox saloon and looked all around at the faces of men scattered about the small drinking hole. Unlike so many other of the town's various saloons the Silver Fox catered mainly for cowboys. Its beer was warm and its whiskey was rugged. Yet it was one of the quieter saloons due to the fact that the gold miners could afford to drink in the more expensive bars.

A rotund man with a waxed moustache finished polishing a glass and smiled at the marshal.

'Howdy, Marshal.'

'Joe.' Matt Fallen nodded and headed to a table.

'What'll it be, Marshal?' the bartender asked.

'Two glasses of whiskey, Joe,' Fallen replied.

Elmer pulled out a chair and sat opposite the marshal as two glasses of dark liquor were brought to the table and placed before them. Fallen handed a silver dollar to the well-rounded figure and then stared at the glass before him.

'Drink up, Elmer.' Fallen lifted the glass and downed the whiskey in one throw. He blinked hard, then carefully placed his empty glass back down. 'Damn! That stuff is rough.'

'Why'd we come in here for, Marshal Fallen?' Elmer asked. He lifted his own glass to his lips and took a sip. He coughed. 'The Silver Fox is known for its mighty powerful rotgut.'

'I came in here to think, Elmer.' Fallen nodded towards the bartender. 'It's quiet in here. There's nowhere as quiet as a saloon full of tuckered cowboys.'

'We ain't gonna be able to see if we keep drinking this hooch, Marshal Fallen.' Elmer managed to finish his whiskey as Joe refilled their glasses. 'This whiskey could strip paint off a fence pole.'

'I need to sharpen my wits.' Fallen

downed the second glass and shook his head. 'Wow! Reckon ya right, though. That stuff is a tad potent.'

Elmer sighed heavily and rested his elbows on the table top. He stared at the thoughtful man opposite him. 'There ain't no way that Bruno can ever blame you for what happened to Billy.'

Matt Fallen nodded. 'I hope ya right. He's got a lot of well-paid cowhands who'll do anything he tells them, though. I don't want us caught up in a war.'

'Bruno ain't got the mustard to tackle you.'

'Not straight on but Bruno has a habit of paying top dollar to get other men to do his dirty work for him,' Fallen replied. 'I'm still surprised he ain't hired another gunslinger after Texas Tom failed to earn his blood money.'

'Bruno's loco,' Elmer said.

'That's what troubles me,' the marshal drawled. 'Ain't easy to figure out what a man will do next when he's loco. Now he's gonna be grief-stricken *and* loco. That's a damn dangerous combination.'

The deputy clicked his fingers and leaned across the table.

'I just remembered. I found a Bar Q cow-puncher when ya was in with Doc,' Elmer said. 'I sent him to tell Bruno the bad news.'

'Then we have about an hour before Jackson gets to War Smoke, Elmer,' the marshal estimated. 'After that who knows what'll happen?'

'I'm sure nothing bad will happen, Marshal Fallen,' Elmer said, and bit his lip. 'Even Bruno can't be dumb enough to think that you killed Billy when you was here in town and Billy had to have been shot out on the trail someplace.'

'I hope ya right.'

'So do I.'

Fallen stood and looked around the saloon at the faces of the cowboys. Most of them were from other ranches but every one of them looked at the big lawman in the same way. They did not trust anyone with a tin star pinned to his vest.

'Let's go have us some supper and

51

then check back to Doc,' the marshal suggested. 'I figure we got us a long night ahead of us when Jackson gets here with his top hands. There won't be any time for us to get any shut-eye.'

'I reckon ya right, Marshal Fallen,' Elmer agreed. He stood up, leaving his second glass of whiskey on the table. 'A steak would go down real well if'n you're paying.'

'I'm paying. C'mon.' Fallen touched his hat brim to the bartender and led the way back out into the cool evening air.

The night stage came rolling in to Front Street, drawing both men's attention as it stopped outside the stagecoach depot.

Both men were about to cross the street when they saw the shotgun guard wave at them frantically. Fallen and Elmer walked along the boardwalk and reached the coach as the guard clambered down to the ground.

'Marshal Fallen?' the man asked, cradling his scattergun in his arm as if it were a baby. 'Are you Marshal Fallen?'

'Yep,' the marshal answered.

'I got me some news to tell ya,' the guard said anxiously.

'Then spill it, stranger,' Fallen demanded.

The guard stepped closer and looked up at the face of the lawman. He seemed nervous.

'The deputy over at Cougar Bluff told me to warn ya,' the guard began. 'He said that Kid Fury is heading this way. He tried to wire ya but the telegraph man said that the wires are down between here and there.'

'Who in tarnation is Kid Fury?' Elmer asked innocently.

'There ain't no paper on him,' Fallen said confidently. 'If he was wanted I'd sure know about it.'

The guard rubbed his whiskers. 'There was a gunfight back in Cougar Bluff. The sheriff was gunned down when he tried to stop a fight. Kid Fury was involved somehow.'

'Did he shoot the sheriff?' Marshal Fallen asked.

The guard shrugged. 'I don't know. All I know is that he rode out on a grey pony and was said to be heading here.'

'Is he a gunfighter?' Elmer asked.

'Sure sounds like one,' Matt Fallen said thoughtfully.

The stagecoach guard gave out a long sigh. 'Folks say he's a real short varmint. Fast on the draw, though. If ya run up against him don't be fooled by his lack of size.'

Elmer raised an eyebrow and nodded. 'Them short ones are always the worst, Marshal Fallen. They get all fired up on account of everyone being taller than them.'

The guard gave another shrug. 'Well, I did my duty and I told ya what that deputy asked me to tell ya, Marshal. I gotta get on with my job now.'

'I'm much obliged.' Fallen touched his temple as if in salute, then led his deputy away from the stagecoach.

'This Kid Fury critter sure sounds like he's a real troublesome kind of varmint, Marshal Fallen.' Elmer gulped as he looked around at the still busy street. There were riders still entering the town from all directions as men from outlying ranches came to War Smoke to gamble, drink or womanize. 'He could be any of these critters that are coming and going. Glory be. Kid Fury might already be here in town.'

'Could be.'

'What if he's a hired gun?' Elmer queried. 'Bruno might have sent for him to come here and draw down on ya, or even worse. He might be a back-shooter.'

Matt Fallen dismissed all of the deputy's theories and set off across the street towards one of the many cafés. 'Are ya coming, Elmer?'

'Ya still buying us steaks?'

'Yep.'

The deputy ran after the tall figure as Fallen reached the café and took hold of the door handle. Both men entered the aromatic interior of the small, one-room eatery. The marshal sat next to the window and looked out into the lantern light. He studied everything and everyone that passed the window.

'What ya thinking about, Marshal Fallen?' Elmer asked as he waved at the cook. 'Steak?'

The marshal shook his head and eyed his deputy.

'Nope,' he drawled. 'Kid Fury.'

4

There was a sense of strange foreboding throughout War Smoke. Since the arrival of the dead cowboy a fearful rumour had started to spread like a wildfire. Every person within the town's unmarked boundaries had started to speculate that once again their intrepid marshal was drawing hired gunmen like flies to an outhouse. Whenever folks got themselves murdered in or around War Smoke it was usually nothing more than a smokescreen and every one of the townspeople knew it.

Matt Fallen was the true target.

He was always the target.

Billy Jackson was a pitiful warning of what was yet to come. Death had returned to the remote town and it would not be satisfied with just one victim, they all gossiped.

An hour had passed since four sturdy

men had carried the body of young Billy into Doc Weaver's parlour, but to each of the town's worried people it felt as though far less time had elapsed.

Then, almost unnoticed at the very edge of town, a slim, handsome Appaloosa stallion laden down with an arsenal of weaponry walked out from the darkness and into the side streets. The lantern light spilled fleetingly across the valuable horse as it was guided ever closer to the heart of the town by its rider. Notorious gunfighter Waco Walt Dando was perched high on its high Mexican saddle and was confident that there were few other horses as tall as his three-year-old mount. It gave him an unrivalled view of everything his merciless eyes wished to observe.

Waco Walt seldom ventured far from his normal killing ground, but when his high price was not only met but bettered he would ride anywhere. The hired gunman was as lean as the horse he rode and seemed to be staring far ahead from beneath his flat-brimmed black hat.

As the magnificent horse took one long-legged stride after another the rider did not appear to move a muscle. He continued to look far ahead of them to some distant point that only he knew of. As with so many of his profession Waco Walt knew when and how to kill so that he earned his blood money and never fell foul of the law. But when the law was not looking he would kill anyone who got in his way. As long as there were no witnesses the gunfighter knew he would never pay for his crimes.

The evening was cold and getting even colder but the horseman did not seem to be aware of the temperature as he allowed his stallion to continue forward.

There was something else on his mind.

It was the deadly reason that had brought him hundreds of miles from Waco to War Smoke.

The streets were still busy but now

more and more of the townspeople were finding sanctuary in the warmer saloons and gambling houses. Smoke billowed from every black metal chimney stack throughout the community. The smoke hung like a cloak across the entire town and the air grew even icier as the night progressed on its inevitable course.

The horseman reached Front Street from a side alley, eased back on his reins and stopped the impressive animal. The slim Appaloosa rested as its master surveyed the wide street before him. His eyes were like slits cut into his face. They moved unseen behind the hooded lids.

Nothing escaped the rider's notice. Waco Walt knew only too well that men who lived by the gun, as he did, often died by it. He never took anything for granted because that was a sure path to Boot Hill.

He studied each and every man, woman and even child who still happened to be braving the severe drop in temperature as the night grew older. Any one of them might be his undoing, he thought. All it took was a gun and the courage to pull on its trigger. An avenging brother, father or wife could kill as easily as those skilled in gunplay.

He was like an eagle.

He saw everything. Waco Walt never became complacent when it came to the faces of those who might be grieving for someone he might have killed.

Suddenly the noise of chains rattling drew his well-honed attention. He tilted his head and peered from under the brim of his hat down the long street.

A stagecoach with a six-horse team moved away from the depot a few hundred yards from him. The sound of a whip cracking echoed off the wooden and red-brick walls that surrounded the Appaloosa rider.

He held his mount in check as the long vehicle came clattering along the street towards him. He did not move or allow his horse to move until the stagecoach passed the alley in which he waited. Dust kicked up into the frosty air.

Although the street was filled with lanterns none of their light touched the horseman or his mount. He had found the blackest of shadows to rest in and remained there as his keen eyes continued to search the faces of those who innocently walked past him.

As the dust from the hoofs and wheel rims of the stagecoach settled back on to the sandy surface of the street the horseman tapped his long spurs and steered his mount into Front Street.

Waco Walt had never seen a town quite so busy after sundown before, but he had never been in one set close to gold mines. The light from numerous storefronts spilled at intervals across the sand to both sides. The gunfighter guided his mount to the very centre of the wide street in a vain bid to escape their betraying illumination.

His hooded eyes burned through the smoke, which floated in the air like a gathering of phantoms, in search of his goal. Waco Walt was looking for the place where he had been instructed to meet the man who had sent for him.

At the furthest end of the street he could see the activity around the many saloons and gambling halls. Blazing torches buried into the ground outside their brightly painted façades were drawing the townspeople like moths to naked flames.

The deadly gunfighter knew that that was where he would find the building he was seeking. The closer he rode the clearer the names became to his unblinking eyes.

Every painted name that he studied seemed to be more elaborate than the previous one. Each seemed designed to be more boastful than its neighbour, but only one of the names on the wooden façades interested the gunfighter sitting high atop the Mexican saddle as the Appaloosa walked slowly through the crowd towards it.

The Dice.

The horse proceeded at a steady pace towards the gambling hall set amid so many other similar businesses. That was his destination: the reason for which Waco Walt Dando had ridden so far and was now in the remote town called War Smoke.

Yet even as Waco Walt approached he had no idea who or what to expect when he eventually entered its imposing four walls, for he had accepted the blood money without question.

It had never mattered to the ruthless hired killer who his next victim might be. All he had ever considered was that his price was met.

Fifty yards from where the gunfighter was steering his mount through the crowd two men emerged from a side street and paused opposite Doc Weaver's house. Matt Fallen and his deputy had finished their supper an hour earlier and had again done the rounds of the sprawling town. They were about to cross the wide street when the marshal stopped abruptly upon seeing

Waco Walt. His honed instincts knew trouble when they set eyes upon it. It was a troubled Fallen who bit his lip as he watched the rider.

'Why'd ya stop so sudden, Marshal Fallen?' Elmer asked. He stepped out from behind the broad-shouldered lawman and stumbled off the board-walk. 'I almost bumped into ya with my scattergun.'

Fallen raised a finger and pointed down the street at the approaching rider. Front Street was still busy and filled with the steam from two- and four-legged creatures alike. This, mixed with the chimney smoke trapped in the icy night air, cast an eerie veil over everyone in the long thoroughfare.

'Who do ya figure that is, Elmer?' the marshal asked, rubbing his jaw thought-fully. 'I ain't seen him before.'

Elmer squinted. 'Who are ya aiming ya finger at?'

The taller man sighed and slapped the back of his underling's head. 'I'm pointing at the stranger on top of that tall Appaloosa, Elmer. Have ya ever set eyes on him before?'

The deputy shrugged. 'No, I ain't ever seen him in War Smoke before. I'd sure recall seeing a critter like him. He surely looks mean, Marshal Fallen.'

Matt Fallen gave a nod of silent agreement.

'We gonna tackle him?' Elmer asked eagerly. 'He might be the critter who shot young Billy. I reckon we should throw him in one of our cells for the night. Look at how many rifles he's got strapped to his saddle. That ain't no drifter.'

'It ain't a crime to have a lot of rifles. Besides, it looks like he headed into town from the opposite direction to Billy, Elmer,' Fallen remarked.

'But he could have ridden all the way around town to make us think he come from thataway instead of thataway,' the deputy reasoned, pointing the barrel of his shotgun in both directions. 'He might even be that Kid Fury critter the stagecoach guard told us about.'

'I sure doubt that.' Fallen shook his head. 'Whoever he is he don't look like no 'kid' to me.'

'Me neither. He is kinda grim-faced now ya mention it,' Elmer admitted. 'Plumb ugly and no mistake.'

Marshal Fallen watched the horseman stop at a hitching rail outside The Dice gambling hall and dismount. Waco Walt wrapped his reins around the rail, stepped up on to the boardwalk and entered the gambling hall.

'I wonder who that critter is going to meet?' Elmer wondered aloud.

The marshal nodded. 'He might be just anxious to lose himself a few bucks.'

'I guess.'

The tall lawman tapped his deputy's arm.

'C'mon, Elmer. Let's go see if old Doc's found any clues to who killed Billy.'

Both men started across the busy street to where they could see lamplight escaping around drawn window drapes.

With each step Fallen continued to look down the street at the well-illuminated gambling house.

They were no more than halfway across the wide street when another horseman appeared from out of the icy mist. Kid Fury trotted his small grey pony behind the two lawmen, keeping a firm grip on his reins.

Elmer turned full circle as his eyes followed the rider before the Kid merged into the crowd and disappeared from view. The deputy then swung on his heel and grabbed Fallen's arm.

'Did ya see him, Marshal Fallen? Did ya?'

The tall lawman gave a slow nod.

'Sure I saw him. It was just a young kid on a grey pony.' As the words left his lips the marshal suddenly realized what he had said. The marshal turned and stared along the busy street and repeated, 'A kid on a grey pony. Could that have been Kid Fury?'

'Glory be!' Elmer gasped. 'I ain't never seen that young 'un before and I knows most of the critters in War Smoke. Do ya reckon that's Kid Fury, Marshal Fallen? He sure ain't very big.'

'Maybe he is and maybe he ain't.' Fallen walked on towards Doc Weaver's house with his excited deputy a few steps behind him. 'I got a feeling we'll find out soon enough.'

5

Waco Walt Dando looked around the lavish trappings of the spacious foyer and the well-dressed patrons of The Dice with nothing but disgust. He ambled towards a desk where a huge, barrel-chested man stood with his arms folded. The man was paid to prevent anyone whom he considered to be unworthy from entering the gambling hall.

'Get out,' the large man snarled at Waco Walt.

The gunfighter stood across the desk from the man and said nothing. He lowered his chin until it touched the knot in his bandanna and gave out a long sigh.

'Is ya deaf?' the huge man snapped. 'I told ya to vamoose and I meant it. Get going.'

Waco Walt pushed the brim of his hat

back to reveal the slits he had for eyes and gave a sickening grin. His long-fingered hands then lowered and pulled the sides of his trail coat back to reveal his matched pair of six-shooters. His hands hovered above the grips. He saw the expression on the face of the man behind the desk change. Suddenly the doorkeeper realized that this was no drifter covered in the caked dust of a long ride, but a very different breed of creature.

This was a man who lived by the gun.

'I'm here to meet somebody,' Waco Walt said in a low, rasping whisper. 'I'm here and I ain't going anywhere until I meet him.'

The big man seemed suddenly to shrink; he felt beads of sweat trail down his face. He was looking straight into the hooded gaze of a creature who he knew could kill him in a mere blink of an eye.

'Who are ya here to meet?' the doorkeeper stammered.

'I don't know his name,' Waco Walt hissed in reply. 'He knows me, though. He sent for me. He wants me to do a job for him.'

The man behind the desk swallowed hard. 'I don't understand, stranger. How can I get him for ya if we don't know his name?'

The gunfighter stepped closer to the desk. His hands still hovered over his pearl-handled gun grips.

'He knows my name. Why don't ya just head on in to the main gambling rooms and call my name out. He'll come and find me.'

'What's ya name?'

'Walt Dando,' the gunfighter whispered. 'Waco Walt Dando.'

'I've heard of you.'

'Then ya know what I do for a living.'

The doorkeeper felt his heart quicken. He had heard the name many times and knew what it meant. It meant he was standing three feet away from a hired killer. A man who, he knew, would probably not think twice about drawing his guns and shooting.

'I'll escort ya into the boss's private office,' the barrel-chested man said. He managed to force his legs to walk away from the desk. He gestured to a door with the word 'Private' painted upon its varnished surface. He opened the door. 'Wait in here and I'll go and see if I can find the man who sent for you, Mr Dando.'

Waco Walt gave a nod and entered the room.

'Bring a bottle of whiskey back with ya. I got me a lot of trail dust to wash out of my damn throat. Being sober makes me ornery.'

'Sure thing.' The doorkeeper shut the office door, then closed his eyes. Grateful that he was still alive, he inhaled deeply until he managed to stop his large frame from shaking. He then marched into the heart of the gambling hall and prayed that he could find the man who had sent for the notorious gunfighter.

6

None of the alluring females or brightly painted façades the young horseman passed tempted Kid Fury. It was hard to be tempted when you were down to your last couple of bucks. The Kid had ridden to the far end of Front Street when he noticed out of the corner of his eye a small, drab hotel set in a side street just off the main thoroughfare. He eased back on his reins and turned the pony. His eyes screwed up and he peered along the dimly lit street, which was in total contrast to the rest of War Smoke. It was barely wider than an alley. He steered his grey pony up through the shadows, drew rein outside the Parker Hotel and dismounted.

There were no hitching poles in the street but there were plenty of porch uprights. He looped the long leathers around the one closest to the double

74

doors and secured it firmly. The young man checked his pockets, found what remained of his last wages and nodded to himself. He had learned to be frugal long ago, for sometimes money was hard to come by. Contrary to what his reputation implied, Kid Fury did not hire out his gun skills to the highest bidder. He placed the six coins into his vest pocket and looked around him. This must be the poorest part of War Smoke, he reasoned, but at least it was within his meagre budget.

He had enough to rent a room for a couple of days, leaving some over to keep his mount at the livery. As long as he did not eat too much he might last until he could earn a few honest dollars.

The Kid stepped up on to the boardwalk, turned the door handle and entered the small rooming house.

There were no fancy trimmings in the Parker Hotel. A solitary candle burned on a saucer near a register upon the crude desk. There was an uncarpeted staircase and a grubby door in need of a coat of paint just behind the desk. This was a hotel by name only. An average-sized house that rented rooms to those who could not afford the high prices of its Front Street counterparts.

The small desk looked as though it had been constructed from old packing cases. Kid Fury moved towards it and looked around for any sign of life. The flickering light from the candle spoke volumes to the youngster. He knew all about hard times. He knew that there were many folks who could never afford either to buy a lamp or the coal oil to put in it.

A floorboard creaked above his head. He looked up at the cobwebbed ceiling and stepped closer to the foot of the stairs.

'Hello?' he called out. 'Is anybody here?'

The Kid listened to the movement up on the landing as footsteps responded to his query. He stepped back to the desk and looked down at the open register, filled with names that he was unable to read. The sound of gentle steps descending the staircase made him turn. To his total amazement he saw the most beautiful young female he had ever beheld. Although dressed in clothes that confirmed her poverty she was utterly breathtaking. She was barefoot and beautiful.

The Kid tried to work out how old she might be. All he knew for sure was that she must be a little younger than he was. There was a bounce in her step as she floated down towards him, which made his heart race. Although the light from the candle was poor it seemed to find every beautiful feature of her face and body. The light of a thousand lamps could not have done her any more justice.

She smiled when she saw him. For the first time in his entire life Kid Fury actually felt as if he had just set eyes upon the most perfect female in the world.

Perhaps he had.

His heart was pounding as she

moved effortlessly around the desk and rested her small hands upon its surface. She was still smiling and the Kid felt his cheeks redden.

'Ya want a room?'

Her voice matched her looks, he thought. It was sweet, like honey. He removed his Stetson as if somewhere in the back of his mind he had been reminded of long-forgotten manners. He held the hat over his chest and bowed respectfully.

'Yep. I'm looking for a room for a few nights, ma'am.'

'That'll be ten cents a night.' She grinned.

'I'll be staying for two nights, ma'am.' Kid Fury pulled out two dimes and gave them to her.

'My name's Angie,' she informed him, looking even more intently into his boyish face. 'What they call you?'

He could not think as he stared at her. He had never seen a face so pretty. He had never seen hair as golden brown. It was like being in the presence of a princess. A princess in rags.

'What's ya name?' Angie repeated softly.

'They call me Kid Fury.' He sighed.

Her perfect eyebrows rose towards her fringe. 'That ain't ya real name, is it?'

Without even realizing it he shook his head. 'My real name's Jim. Jim Fury. Everybody calls me Kid, though, on account of me being little.'

Angie Parker's head tilted but her eyes remained focused upon the young man before her. 'Ya ain't that little, Jim. Ya taller than me.'

The Kid smiled. 'I reckon there can't be a whole lot of folks that ain't taller than you, Angie.'

She turned the register to face him, licked the tip of a pencil and handed it to him. 'Ya have to sign this.'

He accepted the pencil.

'You sure are pretty,' Kid Fury said as he made his mark.

Angie looked at the crude cross on the book and suddenly realized that the handsome young man with the expensive shooting rig strapped around his hips was incapable of writing his own name.

'And you're real sweet, Jim.' Angie blushed.

Kid Fury was given a room key. He nodded and looked at it before returning his eyes to the beautiful young female before him. He could not conceal his interest in her.

'I'd ask ya if there was a chance of you stepping out with me, Angie,' he stammered nervously. 'Trouble is I ain't got a whole lot of money until I get me a job.'

She looked at him in a way that she had never looked at any man before. She felt something inside her which she did not understand but liked. It was a warm feeling. It was as though she had just met a long-lost friend, even though they had never encountered one another before.

'Ya don't need money to step out with someone, Jim,' she said in a low, soft tone. 'There's a whole lot of things that don't cost anything at all.'

Kid Fury felt his heart quicken. 'Maybe ya might show me?'

Suddenly the door behind Angie swung open and a dishevelled man holding a glass of whiskey emerged. He looked as if he had been drinking for most of the previous few decades as his bloodshot eyes glared at the young stranger.

'You even touch my little daughter and I'll have ya run out of town on a rail, boy. Savvy?' Ben Parker threatened as he shook a fist across the desk.

'Don't be like that, Pa,' Angie begged.

Ben Parker pushed her aside and continued to wave his fist under the nose of Kid Fury. Her eyes began to fill with tears.

'Shut ya damn mouth, girl,' Parker snarled drunkenly. 'Ya mother was a filthy whore and I sure ain't gonna let you become the same. Not for the first cocksure drifter that rents a room, anyway.'

'That ain't no way to talk to ya

daughter, *amigo*,' Fury said in a low growl.

'I don't need no lessons from a saddle tramp,' Parker said, and downed his whiskey. 'Ya keep ya eyes and ya hands off her or there'll be trouble, boy. Big trouble.'

Every inch of the younger man wanted to teach Ben Parker a real lesson, but he could see that the beautiful female was already distressed enough. He did not wish to make matters worse for her.

Kid Fury placed the room key in his shirt pocket, turned reluctantly away from Parker and stepped towards the door. He clutched its handle, turned it, then looked over his shoulder at Angie's enraged father. His eyes burned into the drunken man's soul.

'I'm taking my horse to the livery,' Kid Fury said. 'Then I'm coming back and I'd be obliged if ya didn't harm ya daughter in my absence, mister.'

'Nobody tells me what I can and can't do with my own flesh and blood, boy,' Parker said with a snort. 'Unless ya threatening me. Are ya, half-pint?'

'I never threaten anyone,' the Kid said calmly. 'I just warn critters like you that it don't pay to get me riled. Do ya understand?'

Parker and the Kid stared into each other's eyes. The hotel proprietor was the first to blink and turn away. Kid Fury watched as the man staggered back into the room behind the desk.

'I'm sorry,' Angie whispered fearfully.

'There ain't no call for ya to be sorry.' Kid Fury touched the brim of his hat to Angie. She smiled through her tears. The Kid opened the door and walked out into the dark street. He moved to the upright and pulled his reins free. He stepped into his stirrup and mounted the grey pony.

Sweat ran down the sides of his face. He did not understand the emotion that had overwhelmed him, but he knew that he had come close to drawing his guns and killing the man who, he feared, might have a habit of harming the beautiful girl named Angie.

He checked the few coins he had remaining, then turned the pony. Fury tapped his spurs and urged the horse to start walking into the shadowy depths of War Smoke.

Kid Fury did not know where the nearest livery stable was but he knew his flared nostrils would not have a lot of trouble locating it.

Suddenly the pony shied.

The young rider had to use every ounce of his renowned horsemanship just to remain in his saddle as the pony bucked in fear beneath his saddle. As he steadied himself atop the nervous grey he too heard the sound of a number of approaching horses.

Then the noise became a deafening crescendo of pounding hoofs that echoed off the weathered wooden walls that flanked him.

Kid Fury saw the riders appear from around a corner. They charged straight at the startled youngster.

He hauled back on his long leathers. The grey pony responded and backed up as more than a dozen cowboys drove their mounts past him on their way towards Front Street. The narrow street was filled with dust.

Kid Fury spat the dust from his mouth and watched as the Bar Q riders turned from the side street and thundered into the main thoroughfare. None of them slowed his quarter horse as they leaned from their saddles and rode from view.

The Kid tapped his spurs again and continued his search for a livery stable.

7

Like a small army of single-minded troopers the cowboys spurred their mounts towards their leader's goal: Matt Fallen's office. Every one of the townsfolk raced to safety as the riders charged straight down the middle of the sandy street. The rancher at the head of the dust-caked cowboys was filled with a deadly cocktail of grief and anger. Bruno Jackson wanted answers from the man he hated more than any other. He wanted Fallen to explain to him how and why his only son had been shot dead.

The lantern on the wall outside the office glowed as the cowboys approached at frightening speed. Not one of them hauled rein until the very last moment. The cowboys' horses dug their hoofs into the frosty ground, sending sand flying in all directions as they felt their long leathers being jerked back by their masters.

The Bar Q riders pulled up outside the marshal's office and Bruno Jackson hastily dismounted. The snarling rancher stepped up on to the boardwalk and kicked the unlocked door open. He stared inside the empty office, then turned furiously to face his dust-caked cowboys.

'Damn it all. Fallen ain't here,' Jackson growled like a wounded bear, and moved back to his lathered-up horse. His eyes screwed up as he darted his gaze around the busy street. Vainly he searched for the lawman. 'Where the hell is that big galoot?'

The cowboys turned their horses, each rider looking for the big man with the tin star pinned to his vest.

Jackson moved to his top wrangler. 'Where do ya figure they took Billy, Red?'

'I'd bet on the undertaker's, Bruno,' Red Colt answered, rubbing the dust from his face.

'Go check, Red,' Bruno growled angrily.

Red spurred and galloped through

the lantern light.

Jackson grabbed the arm of another of his men. 'Where do ya figure Fallen is, Bob?'

Bob Bates had no answer. 'That varmint could be anyplace, Bruno. War Smoke is a mighty big town.'

'Go look for him,' Jackson ordered. 'If ya find him drag his sorry backside here. I want me some answers.'

'I'll go see if I can find Fallen,' Bates said.

The cowboy spun his quarter horse around and rammed his spurs into its flesh. The animal galloped away.

Jackson mounted his horse and gathered up his reins. 'I wanna find that damn marshal. Fallen must know why young Billy is dead. I got me a gut feeling he has something to do with it. If I'm right, Fallen's a dead man.'

'I figure ya right, Bruno,' one of his cowboys piped up.

Jackson nodded and drew his reins up in his gloved hands. 'Let's go see if Red has found Billy. Then we'll find that damn lawman.'

The Bar Q riders charged back towards the funeral parlour.

8

The two men stared at one another across the private office as the gunfighter poured himself another tall glass of whiskey and swiftly swallowed half of its contents. His hooded eyes glared across the room at the gambler in the white suit as Dandy Jim Buckley produced a wallet from his inside pocket and opened it.

'Five thousand is a lot of money,' Buckley observed. He took the wad of bills and placed them down on the desk next to the deadly killer. 'Are you worth it?'

'Every penny.'

'I'll pay the same again when the job is done,' the gambler said.

Waco Walt scooped the bills up and looked at them. 'Why would anyone want a lawman killed so bad, Dandy Jim?'

'Fallen has been a thorn in the sides

of every businessman in War Smoke for years,' Buckley said. 'He likes to stick to the rule of law and that cramps folks' style when it comes to making real money.'

'I'd have thought it would have been a lot cheaper just to bribe the son of a bitch,' Waco Walt suggested.

'We've all tried that but he's too damn honest.' Buckley gave out a little chuckle. 'There's nothing worse than an honest lawman in my book. None of us are safe from a man who ain't afraid to arrest anyone he considers to have broken the law.'

Waco Walt nodded.

'How will you do it?' The gambler was curious.

'I've already started.' The gunfighter sighed. 'My spies told me about the bad blood between him and the ranchers before I even got here. So I put a fox in the hen house.'

Buckley moved closer to Waco Walt. 'What do you mean?'

'I shot me a cowpoke who was on his

way to town earlier, just to ruffle a few feathers.'

Dandy Jim laughed. 'I wondered about that.'

'Nice doing business with ya.' Waco Walt folded the wad of greenbacks and pushed them into his pants pocket. He looked across at the elegant figure of Dandy Jim Buckley and downed the remainder of the whiskey. He walked towards the owner of the Golden Garter and smiled. 'Matt Fallen must be a real pain in the neck.'

Buckley stepped away from the office door and looked at the gruesome gunfighter. 'He's stopped a lot of folks from making their fortunes, Waco Walt. It's time he met his Maker.'

The man with the hooded eyes was thoughtful. He rubbed his chin with his long, thin fingers.

'Tell me something. Ain't there nobody in War Smoke with the guts to have done this job for ya, Dandy Jim?' The gunfighter stared down at the shorter man. 'After all, I'm the most expensive critter in my profession still alive.'

'There have been a few who tried to get the better of Fallen,' Buckley admitted.

'What happened to them?'

'All dead.' Dandy Jim Buckley smiled. 'Fallen don't die easy.'

The hired killer grabbed the door handle and turned it. 'I reckon that's gonna change real soon, Dandy Jim. I ain't ever failed to honour my promises. Besides, Fallen will be so busy fending off cowboys he ain't even gonna notice me coming after him.'

Dandy Jim Buckley watched as the hired killer pulled the door towards him.

'A word of advice to you. Marshal Matt Fallen is a mighty dangerous lawman, Waco Walt. Don't underestimate him or you'll regret it.'

The gunfighter glared at Buckley. 'Don't go fretting about me, Dandy Jim. He'll be dead by sunup. Then I'll be back for my bonus.'

'I'll be mighty pleased to pay it.'

9

A maze of dark alleys led in all directions but the light from Front Street guided the young Kid Fury towards it like a beacon. In total contrast to the wide, brightly illuminated heart of War Smoke it seemed as though even the moon could not penetrate the alleyways and narrow side streets.

The Kid had left his pony in the livery stables just behind The Dice gambling hall and was cutting down the alley between the gambling hall and the Mustang saloon. He was headed back towards Front Street and knew that from there he would be able to find his hotel in the unfamiliar town.

The pungent aroma of outhouses made the dark alley an even more unpleasant place to walk through than it would otherwise be. Kid Fury had never liked shadows. Trouble and danger tended to fester amongst them, awaiting the unwary.

Without even realizing it the Kid rested his hands on the grips of his holstered guns as he continued to walk back towards the light. He was ready for anything apart from the sight that suddenly greeted his narrowed eyes.

At the very corner of The Dice a magnificent horse stood awaiting its ruthless, deadly owner. A bright street lantern bathed it in amber light. The Kid knew that there were never two horses of its breed with the same markings. Each animal was unique.

The sight of the tall Appaloosa stallion with its distinctive livery and arsenal of weaponry stopped the Kid in his tracks. He had never imagined that he would set eyes upon that horse again.

Then, before Kid Fury had time even to recollect that he had last seen this horse two years earlier, when its master had left him for dead, the tall, lean gunfighter emerged from the gambling hall and started to check his cinch strap.

The appearance of Waco Walt chilled the youngster to the very marrow of his bones. The hired killer was the only man ever to have out-drawn him and the only man ever to have wounded him in all the years the young Fury had been travelling through the Wild West.

A fear such as he had never felt before flowed like a tidal wave through Kid Fury as the memory of their previous encounter filled his young mind.

The youngster was frozen to the spot by the sight of the unmistakable Waco Walt and his equally unique mount. There was only thirty feet between them. Half the distance that there had been when the Kid had tasted the agonizing pain tearing through his left arm two years before.

Fury recalled how he had vainly tried to stop the merciless slayings that Waco Walt had been dishing out. He remembered the unexpected speed displayed by the man with the slits that he called eyes in his face.

No man had ever drawn a gun and fired it with such accuracy or deadly resolve. Kid Fury had only survived because luck had been on his side that day. Every moment of their last encounter was branded into his brain.

He rubbed his left arm as he watched Waco Walt checking his arsenal of rifles strapped on to the Mexican saddle. The arm still ached as a constant reminder of the bullet that had ripped it apart.

The brutal memory of that last meeting blazed inside Kid Fury's brain. He could not shake it off as every sickening second of it exploded inside his head. He had tried and failed to stop the determined hired killer from earning his blood money.

He remembered feeling his left arm being almost torn from its socket by the power of the bullet. The Kid shuddered as he recalled falling from the high rocks he had mistakenly thought would protect him. The pain still lingered. He had crashed into a deep ravine and Waco Walt had never entertained any notion that the youngster could be anything other than dead.

It had taken Kid Fury three months to recover from his injuries, and the scars were not just on his mutilated arm, but were buried deep in his soul.

For the second time since he had entered War Smoke the Kid wanted to kill. In all of his brief life he had never felt the way he had felt since entering the strange town. The drunken man who, it was obvious, abused his beautiful daughter had brought him close to violence a short while earlier and now the haunting memories of what he had seen Waco Walt do to innocent witnesses had lit a fuse in Kid Fury that he had not realized he possessed.

He managed to take a step, then he stopped again as his gaze burned through the distance between them.

Waco Walt had not altered one bit in

the two years since the Kid had locked horns with him. He still looked exactly the same: a cold-blooded hired gun who did other men's killing for them if the price was right. He had not aged one bit.

They say the Devil looks after his own.

For the first time Fury believed it.

The alley was pitch black, for nobody wasted lantern light in the gaps between buildings. Kid Fury knew that Dando could not see him, but the youngster could see the deadly assassin clearly.

For too many years the Kid had been forced to use his matched .44s just to remain alive, but even though he was faster than most when it came to drawing them from their holsters, he had been no match for Waco Walt.

At least, he had not been on the previous occasion when the two men had met. A thought flashed through Kid Fury's mind. What if he were forced into another showdown with the notorious hired gunslinger?

Would the outcome be even worse?

Would Waco Walt manage to kill him this time? There was a slender chance that if they were to have another show-down the gunfighter might have lost some of his legendary speed with his guns, Fury thought.

That was a real slender chance, though. Thinner than a cigarette paper.

Kid Fury mustered up every scrap of his youthful courage before he resumed walking towards the man who he knew killed anyone he was paid to kill.

A thousand thoughts raced through his mind as he kept walking towards the creature he feared more than any other. He knew he had to try and stop the man, who must be here in War Smoke for only one reason.

There was no one else who knew the truth.

It was up to him. Whatever the possible outcome, he had to try.

Suddenly the tall gunfighter pulled his reins free of the hitching rail and grabbed his saddle horn. He stepped into his stirrup and swung his leg over his saddle. Like some demonic phantom Waco Walt whipped and spurred his mount. The Appaloosa responded and galloped away from the corner.

The Kid raced to the brightly lit street and stared at the dust as people continued to walk in all directions between the youngster and the treacherous killer.

'Damn!' Kid Fury cursed angrily.

Then a sickening realization came to him.

Waco Walt was riding hard and fast in the direction of the side street and the drab hotel.

A sudden panic overwhelmed the youngster. What if the beautiful Angie innocently got in Waco Walt's way? Kid Fury knew that the lethal gunfighter never showed any mercy to anyone who got between him and his chosen prey.

The Kid jumped up on to the trough and looked over the heads of the people who filled the length of the street between himself and the now distant rider.

The distinctively marked rump of the tall stallion made it easy to pick out even in a crowd of other horses. Fury narrowed his eyes and saw Waco Walt steer his mount into the very side street that he himself had left only ten minutes before.

'No!' The Kid leapt down to the ground. 'Angie.'

He started to run.

10

The merciless Waco Walt steered the elegant Appaloosa stallion into the shadowy side street and aimed it straight at the weathered building with the word 'Hotel' painted upon the side wall. The horseman looked all around him, and when satisfied that there was no one within view he dismounted. He secured his reins, then stepped up to the front door and opened it. Within a mere heartbeat he had entered and closed the door behind him. His hooded eyes darted around the cramped area as he stepped closer to the open register and rested a hand upon its pages.

Waco Walt stared at the door just behind the desk. The cursing voice from beyond its flaking paintwork was well known to the hired killer.

'Ben,' the deadly gunman shouted at the door.

The ranting voice ceased. There was the sound of movement, then the door opened.

Waco Walt stared at the familiar face of a man with whom he had once ridden. He barely recognized him. The once deadly gunfighter who had rivalled Waco Walt himself was now a mere drunken shell of his former self.

The tall gunfighter was about to speak when his keen eyesight spotted the young female behind Parker. She was bleeding from belt marks on her tiny back and trying to pull her ragged clothing over her in a vain attempt to conceal her modesty.

'Waco,' Parker slurred. He staggered to the desk and rested both his hands upon it to steady himself.

The gunfighter did not know exactly what he had interrupted but he had a good idea. He lowered his head and looked at his old partner long and hard.

'Ya knew I was headed here,' Waco Walt said. 'I wired ya to tell ya when I was gonna arrive. Didn't ya get the wire?'

Ben Parker exhaled. The smell of his putrid breath caused the gunfighter to back off.

'Sure I got it. I'm ready.'

Waco Walt shook his head. 'What happened to ya? Ya don't look able to help me. I don't need a drunk on my payroll.'

'I ain't a drunk.' Parker clenched his fist and went to throw it at the chin of the deadly hired killer. He was far too slow to achieve even that simple feat.

Faster than a sidewinder could strike with venomous fangs, Waco Walt Dando grabbed the fist in his own more powerful hand and squeezed it hard. He saw Parker buckle in pain.

'Don't ya ever try to strike me, Ben. I ain't no little gal that can be whipped. I'll kill ya damn quick if the mood suits me.'

'Let go,' Parker squealed like a stuck pig.

The gunfighter released his grip and watched as Parker tried to gather his wits.

'We rode together for three years, Ben,' Waco Walt said in a low growl. 'Back then there weren't many who could outdraw either of us. Look at ya now. Ya just a shabby old man who beats on little gals.'

'That's my daughter,' Parker told him. 'I got the right to beat on her. How else is she gonna learn?'

'Learn what?' Waco Walt asked. He grabbed hold of the unsteady figure and forced him back into the small room. The tall gunfighter's eyes darted around the candlelit room and saw Angie cowering in the corner. He pushed Parker down on to a chair and looked straight at her. 'Get out of here, gal. Don't ya go coming back here until dawn. Me and ya pa got important private things to discuss.'

Angie did not require telling more than once. She pulled her torn clothing over her bruised and bleeding body and raced out of the room.

Waco Walt watched as she left the drab hotel, then he pushed the door shut. He levelled his eyes at the drunken man and shook his head.

'I need ya to do a job for me tonight, Ben,' Waco Walt told his old partner. 'I need a distraction. Do it right and I'll pay ya more money than ya ever seen before. Do it wrong and I'll kill ya like the mangy dog that ya are. Savvy?'

Ben Parker nodded. 'I savvy, Waco.'

Waco Walt leaned over Parker and slapped the unshaven face. 'Now sober up.'

11

The surface of the side street was white with frost, which had started to harden the normally soft sand. The terrified young female was standing beside the tall Appaloosa, trying to cover her bruised and bleeding flesh with what was left of her ripped dress and shawl. Angie was shivering with cold when she heard the sound of running growing louder. It echoed off the wooden walls to either side of her tiny form. The tall horse stood between her and whoever was approaching, blocking her view. Angie was unafraid, for she knew that the only true danger she ever faced was inside the hotel. No one outside the hotel's four walls had ever harmed her the way her father had done repeatedly over the years.

Angie stepped cautiously away from the stallion and stared through the shadows at Kid Fury racing as fast as his legs could carry him towards her. A sense of unimaginable relief filled her as she ducked under the tethered reins and approached the panting young man. The smile returned to her pretty face, although she was totally unaware of it.

For some reason she held her arms out to him and he found them. The Kid came to an abrupt halt and dropped his brow on to the top of her soft, fragrant hair. He was not used to running and it showed.

'How come ya running, Jim?' her soft voice whispered.

'Thank God. Ya OK,' the Kid said. He wrapped his arms around her and hugged her. 'I was so scared.'

In truth Angie was far from OK. She was hurting from the punishment her father had inflicted upon her only minutes earlier. Wide belts on small backs always hurt.

As the Kid released his grip on her petite body he saw her tear-filled eyes sparkle in the lantern light, which was reflected in the windows of a house behind his shoulders.

She was also wincing.

'What's wrong?' Fury asked. 'Did I hurt ya, Angie? I'm sorry.'

'No, ya didn't hurt me,' she replied.

Kid Fury gritted his teeth and looked at the Appaloosa tied to the same porch upright to which he had secured his own pony earlier. His eyes narrowed.

'Did Waco hurt ya?'

'No. Not him.' Angie tried to turn her face away from his but he held her chin in his hands and saw the truth written in her tears.

'Was it ya pa that hurt ya?' he asked.

She did not reply. She did not have to, for Kid Fury had already read her mind. He had seen how Ben Parker was when he was liquored up.

'Why would anyone hurt his daughter?' he sighed. 'It don't make no sense.'

'Don't tell anybody,' Angie begged.

'I reckon a lot of folks must already know, Angie.' The young man led her to the shadows and kept his arm around her shoulders. For a reason he had yet to fully understand Kid Fury was protecting her from any further harm.

'Is Waco in there?' he asked.

She nodded. 'Yep, he seems to know my pa. He said they had private things to talk about. He told me not to return to the hotel until after sunrise, Jim. I don't understand. Pa never mentioned he knew anyone like him.'

'A lot of folks wouldn't admit to knowing the likes of Waco Walt, Angie,' Fury replied. He continued to stare at the handsome stallion tethered to the hotel porch upright.

'Who is he?'

The Kid frowned. 'Calls himself a gunfighter but he ain't nothing but a hired killer.'

'How does a critter like that know my pa?' Angie was as confused as was the young man she was holding tightly in her bruised arms.

'And what in tarnation would a hired killer want with ya pa anyway?' Fury

111

muttered, and tried to work out the answer to his own question. 'Maybe they're real old friends, or maybe just old cohorts.'

Angie winced again. Tears rolled down her face from her large eyes. The Kid peeled her tattered shawl away from her shoulders and gasped in horror. Even the dark shadows could not hide the sight of blood which stretched across her narrow back from his keen eyes.

'Ya pa whipped ya?' Fury angrily blurted.

'He don't mean to hurt me, Jim,' Angie said, holding his hands in her own. 'It's the whiskey. It makes him angry. It ain't his fault.'

Kid Fury inhaled deeply. 'Nobody makes him drink the stuff.'

'Don't be angry, Jim.'

'I ain't angry.' Fury sighed and touched her cheek. 'I'm real upset. I don't like the thought of anyone hurting ya, Angie.'

She turned to face the concerned Kid and looked into his eyes. They too were glistening, as if he could feel her pain just as she felt it. Her small fingers touched his cheeks and then for some reason she did not fully comprehend she pulled his face towards her own.

Their lips met.

For the first time in either of their lives they felt truly happy. The kiss seemed to last an eternity before they both drew their heads back. They were both staring at one another in blissful ignorance.

'Why'd ya do that?' he asked.

'I don't know.' Angie gulped. 'Do ya mind?'

Kid Fury gave a slight, innocent shake of his head. 'Nope, I liked it.'

'I liked it as well.' Angie smiled.

Then the sound of the hotel door opening filled the narrow street. Faint candle-light framed the wide shoulders of the tall gunfighter as Waco Walt stepped out into the street and moved to his horse.

Kid Fury kept Angie behind him as he watched Waco Walt walk around the Appaloosa to where he had his arsenal of weapons attached to the large Mexican saddle.

'That's him,' Angie said fearfully.

'I know.' The Kid nodded.

'What's he doing?' Angie whispered into the Kid's ear.

'I'm not sure,' Fury answered. 'But I sure intend finding out.'

They continued to watch from the shadows as the deadly hired killer moved to his strange array of hand-tooled scabbards suspended from the high-backed cantle. Waco Walt unbuckled one of the straps and released a brand-new Winchester. The deadly killer then reached into one of the satchels of his saddle-bags and pulled out an unopened box of rifle bullets. The tall man walked back around the handsome stallion, reentered the hotel and closed the door.

'He took one of his rifles,' Kid Fury remarked.

'What for?' Angie asked.

'Why would he do that?' the Kid wondered. 'Something ain't right here,

Angie. In fact I reckon that something is really wrong.'

'What ya mean?'

Fury turned and faced her. He was confused. 'Did ya pa ever talk about what he did before he started running the hotel?'

She shook her head. 'Come to think about it, he's never talked about his past, Jim. Maybe that's why he drinks so much. He might be trying to forget some awful bad things he did.'

'Could be.'

Angie swallowed hard. 'Ya don't think he's gonna shoot my pa, do ya?'

Kid Fury shook his head. 'He'd have used one of his six-shooters if that was his aim. There's only one reason Waco would have taken a rifle and box of shells in there.'

'What?'

There was a long pause before the Kid spoke again.

'He wants ya pa to use that Winchester, for some reason.'

Angie leaned back into the shadows.

'I don't understand.'

'Me neither, Angie.' Kid Fury looked back at the hotel with a renewed urgency. 'But I intend finding out what's going on in the hotel.'

She looked afraid. 'How?'

'I gotta get inside there,' Kid Fury said. 'Trouble is, me and Waco had us a showdown a while back. If he sees me he'll surely start shooting.'

Angie gripped his sleeves and hauled his attention back to her. 'I ain't gonna let ya go in there, Jim. Do ya hear me?'

The Kid was about to argue when he saw an open window just above the hotel porch. He pointed.

'Whose room is that?'

'That's the one I rented to you,' Angie replied. 'I opened the window to freshen it up. Why, Jim?'

The young man stared at the scene opposite them with calculating eyes. The tall horse was tied to the upright just below the lip of the porch overhang. The open window was directly above that.

He rubbed his jaw and nodded.

'It might just work,' he told himself.

'What ya thinking about?' Angie asked the young man whom she had kissed only a few minutes before. 'Ya ain't thinking about doing anything loco are ya, Jim?'

He looked at her beautiful face and smiled.

'I got me an idea,' Kid Fury said.

12

Even the darkest of shadows could not hide the fact that Angie was shivering uncontrollably from the young man who held her tightly in his arms. Their heartbeats became one for the briefest of moments. Gallantly Kid Fury removed his jacket, wrapped it around Angie's tiny shoulders and then looked into her eyes for what he feared might be the last time. There were no words spoken between them. Each knew what the other was thinking. He tilted his head and kissed her again. He had never tasted anything quite so delicious.

She wanted him to remain safe at her side but the young man had other ideas. He knew he would never discover any answers to the questions that were tormenting him unless he faced his fear. He had to get inside the hotel and knew that using the front door was far too dangerous. The bedroom window offered him another choice. A far more preferable one.

'Stay here,' the Kid instructed her as he pulled on his gloves and placed his hat on her beautiful head. 'Whatever ya do, don't come after me coz Waco Walt kills females as easy as he kills menfolk, Angie. Promise me you'll stay here.'

Angie tried to reply but Kid Fury had already raced across the frosty street towards the Appaloosa tied to the porch upright. Her small hands pulled the coat up to her lips. She inhaled his perfume and sighed. The beautiful girl dressed in rags watched him with tearful eyes.

Kid Fury might have been small but he was fast on his feet and agile. He reached the handsome horse, paused and looked up at the porch overhang. It would be no harder than climbing a tree, he told himself. He reached up, took hold of the stallion's saddle horn and stepped into the stirrup.

With the speed that only the young

can summon up he sprang on to the crown of the saddle and stood for a fraction of a second before jumping up and grabbing hold of the edge of the porch overhang.

For a moment he swung like the pendulum of a tall clock from the wooden porch, then, using every scrap of his strength, he hauled his lean frame upwards.

Angie watched with a mixture of awe and excitement welling up inside her heaving bosom as the Kid threw his left leg up on to the porch. With another burst of energy he managed to drag the rest of his body on to the virtually flat roof.

It took only a few seconds for Kid Fury to straighten up and move to the open window. He pulled the soiled lace drapes apart and thrust his right leg into the dark room.

A sliver of moonlight gave illumination. It was all his young eyes required to make out the layout of the unfamiliar ten-foot-square room. Apart from a cot and a small chest of drawers next to it the room was bare.

He looked down. There was no rug on the floor to muffle the sound of his boots from the ears of those below, he thought. He had to be careful. Really careful if he did not want Parker or his deadly guest to hear him advance across the room and make his way out on to the landing.

Making sure that he did not step on to any loose floorboards the Kid made his way across the room and turned the door handle as quietly as possible.

To his relief the door did not squeak as he pulled it towards him. He stared at the dark landing and began to doubt his own judgement. Only a few minutes earlier it had seemed like a good idea to secretly enter the hotel but now the Kid was not so sure.

Kid Fury realized that death could come much faster than any man could run and no heart was strong enough to withstand a bullet. Each step was now going to take him closer to the one man who was capable of bettering him in a shootout. It was not a comforting thought.

Slowly his eyes adjusted and allowed him to see what faced him. There were two other doors on the landing. The further one away was close to the top of the staircase. A rickety rail led from his room straight to it. His gloved right hand guided him along its well-worn surface until he was standing looking down at the small foyer.

Kid Fury paused and looked down at the desk and the flickering candle on the grubby plate set close to the register. He could hear the raised voices of the two men in the room just behind the desk.

Whatever they were saying sounded no clearer than grunts to him. Fury had a choice to make and it did not sit well with him.

He could either return the way he had come and be no wiser, or he could risk his very life, venture down the stairs and try to overhear what the two men were planning.

In his mind the first choice was one that only a coward would make; the second was one which only a fool might even consider. Either way it seemed that he had bitten off far more than he had anticipated.

The gravity of the situation suddenly dawned on the Kid.

Every instinct silently screamed for him to return to the room he had rented and climb back out of the window, but something else told him he had to learn the truth. A man never learned anything by running away from his fear. He had to face it.

He strained to hear what Waco Walt and Parker were discussing, but they were too far away.

The two men might just be old friends having an innocent conversation about old times, he reasoned. They might also be planning something that would leave a lot of dead bodies scattered around War Smoke.

The Kid thought about Waco Walt

and knew the gunfighter never ventured this far away from his home territory unless someone had paid him to kill. That was all the tall gunfighter ever did.

Kid Fury inhaled deeply and started to descend the staircase as carefully as he could. His eyes darted between the bare boards under his boots and the door set just behind the desk.

He eased himself down one step at a time and prayed that none of the boards would betray him. Both his guns remained holstered and even though he could draw them in the mere blink of an eye, Kid Fury was well aware that his old adversary was even faster.

The Kid's heart was pounding inside his chest so hard that it hurt. It had been two years since he had been savagely wounded by Waco Walt, but Fury knew the hooded-eyed gunfighter would instantly recognize him again if he came out of the small room and looked up.

He was halfway down the staircase and the voices were becoming clearer and clearer. The Kid gripped the banister with one hand and maintained his balance by sliding the other down the wall.

The youngster was a sitting duck and he knew it, but he continued his gradual descent. There was no turning back. Kid Fury had made his choice and was stuck with it.

Sweat rolled down his face; his eyes now focused only on the door beyond the desk.

Waco Walt had good reason to kill Kid Fury, the youngster kept telling himself. He had witnessed the hired killer slaying innocent people as well as the person he had been paid to destroy.

The infamous gunfighter had wrongly thought that he had killed the only witness to his bloody outrage; if he set eyes upon him again he would know that he had to finish the job once and for all.

Fury was only three steps from the bottom of the staircase; a closed wooden door was all that separated him from death. A hundred thoughts flashed through his terrified mind as he carefully eased himself down another step.

He recalled why he had never gone to the law and told them what he had witnessed Waco Walt doing two years before. The trouble was that his own reputation was just as soiled as the infamous gunfighter's.

He was Kid Fury. Most folks believed him to be a hired gunfighter as well.

Who would believe Kid Fury's word against anyone else's?

If he had claimed that he had seen Waco Walt brutally murdering innocent people, the gunfighter could have made the same claims against him.

Whom would the law have believed?

It was a risk the Kid had never dared test.

After what had felt like an eternity the Kid reached the ground floor. He inhaled silently and stepped cautiously to the desk. Still he could hear the two men arguing behind the door. He cupped a hand and blew the candle out. He lowered his head and listened harder.

The sound of slapping was mixed with the raised voice of the gunfighter. He was forcing Parker to sober up the hard way, Fury thought. Waco Walt was punching the effects of the whiskey out of the hotel owner, but the Kid still could not understand what the gunfighter required anyone like Parker for. He was a drunk.

What on earth would someone as deadly as Waco Walt need of a man like Parker? The question had only just raced through Kid Fury's mind when, without warning, the door to Parker's private room suddenly swung violently open.

Waco Walt towered over the youngster. 'Kid Fury!'

Kid Fury stared in startled horror down the barrels of two six-shooters clutched in the hands of the tall, monstrous figure of Waco Walt.

'Unbuckle that belt, Kid,' Waco Walt snarled. His long legs stepped towards the smaller man.

'Shoot the kid, Waco,' Ben Parker

said from inside the room. 'He must have heard everything. He'll get us both hanged.'

Waco Walt holstered one of his guns, produced a match from his vest and ran it along the desk. The flame touched the wick of the candle and illuminated the stunned expression on Kid Fury's face.

'This ain't the time to be killing Kid Fury, Ben,' the gunfighter hissed. He shook the match and dropped its blackened wood on to the register. 'That'll come after you and me have done our job. This job gotta be done right so nobody can point a finger at either of us, Ben.'

'Slit his damn throat, Waco,' Parker grunted.

'Nope. When I kill this young pup it'll be real slow, Ben,' Waco Walt replied. A cruel smile etched across his ratlike features. 'I'm gonna enjoy every last bit of killing Kid Fury.'

Kid Fury squared up to the hired gun. His eyes narrowed as he suddenly realized that he no longer feared the man who had haunted his every nightmare for more than two years.

'Ya knew I was here, Waco?' the Kid asked. 'How? I was as quiet as sundown.'

'Yep, I knew ya was here as soon as I stepped into this damn place, Kid,' Waco Walt replied, and rammed the barrel of his gun into the younger man's belly.

'How?'

The gunfighter laughed. 'Ya name's on the damn book here, Kid. Right next to ya mark.'

Kid Fury looked at the register. Although he could not read he could see that Angie had scrawled his name next to the crude mark he had made. She had no way of knowing that by doing so she had alerted his sworn enemy that he had rented a room in this hotel.

'So you've been waiting for me?'

The gunfighter nodded. 'Yep. Now unbuckle that belt.'

The Kid moved one of his hands to his belt buckle as he saw the hideous face of Waco Walt turn to Parker.

'Get a rope and tie this little man up, Ben.'

The youngster hit the gun barrel away from his belly and slammed his gloved fist down on top of the candle. The small foyer was again plunged into darkness as the Kid turned on his heel and started for the stairs. Fury had barely reached the foot of the staircase when Waco Walt leapt like a mountain lion over the crude desk and cracked his .44 across the back of the Kid's head.

The youngster reeled as a blackness engulfed his mind. He staggered like a drunkard, then he was felled by another merciless blow from the gunfighter's gun barrel.

Kid Fury crashed to the floor heavily. Both men loomed over his unconscious body.

'Who is he, Waco?' Parker asked as they lifted the youngster off the floor-boards.

'The one varmint that could get me hanged, Ben,' Waco Walt replied. 'They call him Kid Fury.'

Both men carted the limp Kid into the private room and dumped him on Parker's chair.

'Tie him up, Ben. Then we'll go and put that fox in the hen house like I planned,' Waco Walt snarled.

'Who are ya gonna kill while I'm causing a ruckus, Ben?' the hotel owner asked as he looped strips of rawhide round the feet and hands of the helpless Kid Fury.

The gunfighter wiped the blood off his gun barrel on his trail coat and grinned as Parker moved to his side. He rested a hand on his ex-partner's shoulder.

'Matt Fallen,' he replied.

The colour drained from Ben Parker's face. He rubbed his still aching jaw as the Winchester and a box of bullets were rammed into his hands.

'Ya can't do that, Waco.'

'When the money is right I can kill

anyone I damn well like, Ben,' Waco Walt growled. He led the swaying Parker to the rear door of the hotel. 'And the money *is* right.'

'Who the hell paid ya to kill Fallen?' Parker asked as he was pushed out into the cold, narrow alley.

'Dandy Jim Buckley.'

'Nobody has ever managed to get the better of Fallen, Waco.' Parker shook his head and blinked hard as he stepped into the eerie moonlight.

'I will,' Waco Walt snapped. He raised a finger. He was pointing at the back of the Silver Fox saloon. 'Now get ya worthless hide up there and do like I told ya.'

Parker took a deep breath and tried to gather his thoughts. 'Why'd ya want me to help ya, Waco?'

The tall gunman stepped up to his old partner and stared at him with hooded eyes. He patted Ben Parker's cheek just hard enough to see the fire return to the drunken man's features.

'Even drunk I'll bet ya still the best

132

'That means there was no gunfight,' Fallen said. 'One single shot sounds like an execution. He was ambushed.'

'Who'd ambush a cowpoke?' Deputy Elmer Hook asked.

Doc shook his head. 'Maybe Billy was mistaken for someone else.'

'Did ya cut the bullet out, Doc?'

'I sure did, Matt.' Doc pushed a white enamel kidney bowl towards the marshal. 'That's it.'

'Looks like a .44 to me,' Elmer said.

'That's exactly right, Elmer.'

Fallen rubbed his tired face with his large hands. 'I guess that narrows it down a little. We know that the killer used a .44.'

'Half the guns in town are .44s, Marshal Fallen.'

'I know.' Matt Fallen sighed and stood back up. 'Ya did a good job, Doc. Least-ways ya managed to narrow the possible culprits down to only half the town.'

'Here.' Doc Weaver stood and handed his friend a scrap of paper.

'What's this?'

'My bill.' Doc sniffed as he grabbed his derby and placed it on his shock of white hair. 'Ya owe me two bucks.'

Fallen pushed the paper into his vest pocket, fished out two silver dollars and handed them to his elderly friend.

'Much obliged, Matt.' Doc led the way to the door. 'Come on. Now ya can buy me a drink.'

'Good idea, Doc. I could use a drink.' Fallen placed his Stetson on the dark hair of his head and adjusted his gunbelt.

The three men headed out into the cold street just as two buckboards came thundering into town, full of gold miners. At least a dozen men filled their flatbeds as the vehicles were driven down towards saloons and gambling halls.

'Damn it all! Miners,' Matt Fallen grumbled. 'That's all we need.'

'That sure looks like trouble,' Elmer said as they watched the gold miners eagerly disembark from the buckboards and race into the buildings.

Suddenly two cowboys rode out of a side street close to Doc's house and drew rein beside the tall marshal. Bob Bates and Red Colt looked down at the three men.

'We bin looking for ya, Marshal,' Bates drawled.

'Bruno Jackson ain't happy,' Red added. 'He went looking for the body of young Billy at the funeral parlour and it weren't there.'

Matt Fallen did not utter a word. He just stared up at the pair of Bar Q boys.

'Would ya happen to know where Billy is, Marshal?' Bates asked. 'Bruno got a notion that it was you who killed his boy and he's getting liquored up before he comes to find ya.'

Doc Weaver pushed ahead of the two lawmen and waved a finger at the cowboys. 'Now listen up. Matt didn't have nothing to do with killing Billy. I've got Billy's body in my parlour.'

'What ya got him in there for?' Red asked.

'I cleaned him up and dug the bullet

out,' Doc answered. 'I can tell ya one thing for certain. Billy was shot with a .44. Matt uses a .45. Now go tell Bruno that. I'll be waiting for you boys to bring a buckboard to take him if that's what ya want.'

'We'll go tell Bruno, Doc,' Red said.

'Fine.' Doc snorted.

Red looked at his saddle pal. Both men nodded to one another and turned their quarter horses. They spurred.

'Reckon you'll have to owe me that drink, Matt,' Doc said as he started back to his house. 'I'll wait for them Bar Q boys to come back.'

Matt Fallen rested his hand on his holstered gun. 'We now got a real dangerous mix in town. Miners and Bar Q cowboys and Kid Fury.'

'And I bet that Billy's killer is in War Smoke as well, Marshal Fallen,' Elmer said with a sigh.

'Yeah, I bet ya right,' Fallen agreed.

14

The large moon was directly above War Smoke, set in a cloudless sky. It was getting colder with every passing beat of the hotel owner's black heart. Ben Parker clambered up on the top of the flat roof of the Silver Fox and walked to its very edge.

He stared down into the brightly illuminated street below him with whiskey-fuelled eyes. It was all a sickening blur, but he knew that he had to do what Waco Walt had ordered him to do. There was no option. The lethal hired gunman never allowed anyone to disobey him.

Parker knelt down on the frost-covered roof and opened the box of rifle bullets. They gleamed in the eerie light of the moon. He was panting like an old hound dog after a raccoon hunt. He wanted to sleep off his drink but fear kept him wide awake. No matter how drunk he knew he still was, Parker did not want to disobey his old partner.

He and Waco Walt had ridden together for years on the wrong side of the law. They both had different names back then and had been wanted dead or alive.

It was more than twenty years since the two men had parted company and, with new identities, had managed to create new lives for themselves. Somehow Waco had managed to use his deadly passion for killing to continue to earn a fine living, Parker thought. Yet he himself had taken a far less profitable course and ended up a drunken hotel owner.

Parker rubbed his weary face with the palm of his left hand and studied the busy scene that stretched away in both directions below him. Even drunk he was amazed by how many people were still braving the night. Even the ice-cold weather could not seem to dampen the spirits of the townsfolk as they continued to fill every boardwalk and most of the long street.

One by one he slid the bullets into the Winchester's magazine and cocked the lever. There was no turning back now, Parker's befuddled mind told him. He had to kill just as he had been instructed to do by Waco.

He remembered their outlaw days.

Even then nobody ever challenged Waco. Not without getting their head blown off, anyway. He tried to think of the money he knew Waco Walt would give him when the gunfighter had slain Matt Fallen.

If Waco managed to kill the marshal, that was. It sounded easy enough but no one had ever achieved that feat yet.

Parker screwed up his eyes and tried to focus on the people who filled the street. He wondered where his old partner in crime might be. Front Street was long and straight with countless side streets and alleyways branching off it. He knew the deadly killer could be anywhere.

Waco Walt had always been like a phantom. He tended to find the darkest shadows and then strike when his chosen target least expected it.

The gunfighter was faster than most men with a six-gun but if he could bushwhack his prey, he would. All that had ever mattered to Waco was the money and the sheer pleasure he got from killing.

It had never mattered to Waco whom he gunned down. Any man, woman or child who got in his way or witnessed him murdering an innocent victim would be dispatched to their Maker.

Ben Parker realized that even he was not immune to the deadly retribution of his old partner. Waco was merciless. He would kill anyone.

Nervously Parker pushed the hand guard down and then eased it up slowly. The brand-new Winchester had taken fourteen bullets and was fully primed for action.

He lay down on the ice-cold surface of the roof and stared through his still foggy eyes at the unsuspecting people who milled around the streets.

The trouble was that they all looked like one object to his bloodshot eyes. Parker scraped frost off the roof and rubbed it into his eyelids. His vision temporarily cleared. He could see the gold miners' empty buckboards outside the Golden Garter saloon, then he saw the activity of the numerous cowboys who were riding around in large numbers far below him.

Then his vision faltered again. He could see them but not clearly enough to start picking them off.

Anxiously, Parker rubbed frost into his eyes again in a vain attempt to regain the once perfect eyesight he'd had during his outlaw days. A thought suddenly occurred to him.

What if it was not the whiskey he had consumed earlier that was hampering his ability?

What if his eyesight had succumbed to age, like the rest of his now wrecked body?

Parker rested his temple against the cold steel rifle barrel. He knew he could not start shooting until his vision was clear.

Waco Walt desired dead bodies. A whole lot of dead bodies.

The gunfighter wanted mayhem and confusion to draw the marshal into his well-planned trap. Parker knew that that meant he had to be able to hit what he was shooting at.

'Stay calm, Ben,' he told himself. 'Relax and then ya can start killing. There's enough of them down there for even a blind man to hit a few of the critters with a volley of well-grouped rifle bullets.'

No matter how many times Parker tried to convince his whiskey-fumed brain that he could achieve the goal his old partner had given him, Parker could not stop doubting that his once unequalled marksmanship had forsaken him, like all of his other once abundant attributes.

It seemed to be getting even colder

on the roof. The frost gnawed like hungry rats into his flesh and bones as he tried to get his aching body into a comfortable enough position to start his deadly onslaught.

With shaking blue hands Ben Parker pulled out his tobacco pouch from his vest and extracted a twisted cigarette. He pushed it into the corner of his mouth and scratched a match along the wooden rim of the flat roof. It took three attempts before the match ignited. He cupped the flame in his hands and felt nothing as its flame licked his skin. He eagerly sucked in the smoke until his lungs were filled. His numb fingers dropped the match on to the frost-covered felt. The match hissed like a rattler for a few seconds before a pathetic wisp of smoke rose like a genie into the night air.

He inhaled the smoke deeply. For a moment he held it in his lungs and savoured its strong flavour. Then he slowly let the smoke filter through what was left of his teeth.

He repeated the action and thought about the words of the deadly Waco Walt Dando. Words which described him as being the best damn shot in the West. He had been, before age and whiskey had combined to turn him into the pathetic creature he now was, Parker thought.

'Sober up, Ben. Ya gotta do this before ya freeze to death,' Parker mumbled to himself nervously. Again he tried to rid his eyes of the fog that still hampered him in finding a clear target. 'Sober up fast or there'll be hell to pay.'

15

The narrow side street was becoming bathed in the strange light of the large moon as it slowly crept across the frozen heavens. The shadow that had protected Angie from the eyes of anyone who might have been foolhardy enough to venture along the alley was almost gone. Angie knew that something must have gone wrong for the handsome young man she had kissed about ten minutes ago. She could still taste him on her lips, but with every passing beat of her heart she began to doubt that she would ever be able to kiss him again.

She was afraid. Fear squeezed her mercilessly until she felt she might explode. The frosty night was growing colder, yet she did not notice. Her bare feet were used to the bitter winter nights. She pulled his coat around her and inhaled his scent as her large, beautiful eyes stared at the hotel and the tall Appaloosa stallion tied to one of its porch uprights. The horse, like the tiny female, did not seem to feel the cold.

Angie was becoming more and more troubled by the fact that she had not seen the Kid leave the building, nor had there been any sign of life from either her brutal father or the tall, lethal gunfighter.

Every fibre of her brutalized body told her that something had gone terribly wrong.

She wanted to move forward, but the words of Kid Fury were still in her mind. The Kid had been adamant when he had warned her to remain in the shadows, but now the street was bathed in the betraying light of the overhead moon.

With the coat wrapped around her bleeding shoulders the young female realized that she had to discover the truth.

Grim imaginings flooded through her mind. She had not heard any shots but that did not mean that the handsome and brave young man had not been wounded, or even worse. She knew many ruthless men like Waco often carried murderous knives hidden on their persons when they wanted to kill silently.

As if drawn by unseen strings Angie moved away from the shadows towards the hotel.

He had to be badly hurt, she thought. The Kid would have returned to her by now. The Kid had been in there too long.

Suddenly she felt as though invisible hands were squeezing her throat. A dread filled her small frame. What if he had been caught by the mysterious Waco? What if he were bleeding to death inside the hotel?

She might already have waited too long to help the Kid.

A bead of sweat trailed down her beautiful face in defiance of the freezing temperature, which tortured her already bruised and bleeding body. She was terrified, but she could not remain where the Kid had left her.

Angie had not heard a shot or even a scuffle, she kept thinking, but she knew that that did not mean a thing.

Knives were silent and were also deadly.

Her heart started to beat like a war drum inside her heaving chest as she began to walk faster towards the tall Appaloosa stallion.

The horse was still here.

Did that mean its master was still inside the hotel?

Angie knew that the rear of the hotel led to an alley which ran parallel with Front Street. Waco could have gone out that way to do whatever it was he was intending to do, she thought.

She hesitated beside the stallion as her mind tried to think of what she ought to do. Her fear of her father and of provoking even more of his wrath would normally have kept her outside the hotel. But now there was a driving force inside her heaving bosom. Suddenly Angie was no longer a young girl but a woman with desires that she had yet to truly understand or fulfil. Her love for Kid Fury was far greater than her fear of Ben Parker.

Her small left hand stroked the neck of the high-shouldered horse as she stepped up on to the boardwalk and placed an ear against the front door.

Angie listened and heard nothing.

Again the horrific vision of the Kid lying in a pool of blood filled her thoughts. She trembled.

Angie grabbed the door handle, took a deep breath and, defying her own trepidation, entered. To her surprise and relief the small lobby was empty. A cold blast of air caused the pages of the register to flick over as though being thumbed by unseen hands. Angie clenched her tiny fists and turned.

Her eyes saw that the rear door to the alleyway was ajar.

She rushed across the floorboards, out into the alley and looked around. There was no sign of either Waco Walt or her father. She was about to retrace her steps when her eyes saw the boot-marks on the frosty ground.

Two men had walked in opposite directions away from the back of the hotel, she reasoned. She tilted her head back and then saw the moonlit seated figure up on the roof of the Silver Fox. The moonlight glinted along the long barrel of the rifle in his hands. Then she recognized the rifleman.

'Pa? What ya doing?' she whispered.

Angie rushed back into the house and closed the door behind her. She made her way back to the front of the hotel, then noticed that the door behind the desk was also slightly ajar.

Cautiously she placed her small hand on the flaking paint and pushed it open. The candle flame swayed as she entered the room. Then she saw him.

Kid Fury was lying on her father's chair. He was tightly bound but conscious.

'Jim,' Angie blurted out. She sank to her knees and pulled the crude gag from his mouth. Someone had used the

Kid's own bandanna to muffle his cries for help.

'Angie,' Fury gasped. He watched her untie his hands, then his feet. She was still wearing his hat and it suited her, he silently thought. 'I told ya to stay outside until I came back to ya.'

The light of the candle danced on her smiling face. 'Good job I didn't listen, Jim. I reckon you'd have been here for a couple of days if I'd not come looking for ya.'

Kid Fury got to his feet. 'Yeah, I think ya right.'

'What happened?' Angie stood next to him. 'Who did this?'

He shrugged and felt the bloody wound on the back of his head. He stared at the blood on his fingertips.

'I ain't sure. I tried to make a run for it but Waco was too damn fast for me. I recall him leaping over the desk out there and then everything went kinda black.'

'He must have hit ya with something real hard,' Angie said, looking at the gash on the back of his head.

153

'He did. His gun,' Kid Fury told her. 'I recall him having it in his hand when I tried to make a break for it. He must have lashed out with it.'

'They went out through the alley, Jim,' Angie informed him. She wrapped her arms around his waist. 'One went up on the roof of the Silver Fox saloon and the other kept on going down the alley. What's going on?'

The Kid rubbed his aching head. 'I remember them talking,' he said. 'Waco knocked me out but I started to come to after they'd tied me up. They were talking. What were they talking about? If only I could recall.'

Angie looked into his troubled face. 'Try to remember, Jim. Try.'

Suddenly Kid Fury's expression changed. The colour drained from his face and his eyes widened.

'I remember,' the Kid gasped. 'Waco's been hired to kill the marshal. Ya pa is gonna help him somehow.'

'Ya gotta warn Marshal Fallen, Jim,' Angie pleaded.

He shook his head. 'No. You go and find the marshal. I don't even know what he looks like. You go and find him and warn him. Tell him about ya pa up on the saloon roof. Take Waco's horse and find the marshal.'

'What are you gonna do?' Angie's beautiful eyes looked at the man in her arms.

'The only thing I can do, Angie.' Fury checked both his guns. 'I'm going to find Waco. Find Waco and kill him before he kills the marshal.'

16

'I reckon we'd best go and find Bruno before he finds us, Elmer,' Marshal Fallen told his deputy. 'C'mon.'

'How we gonna find him in them there crowds?' Elmer asked, cradling his scattergun in his arms.

Fallen tapped his nose. 'Find the horse and you'll find the cowboy.'

The lawmen crossed the lantern-lit sand, walking away from Doc Weaver's, when the spine-chilling sound of rapid gunfire rang out. This time it was not a solitary shot but a deafening fusillade of lethal lead, which filled the street. The sound of people screaming in a mixture of pain and terror filled the ears of Matt Fallen and Elmer. Suddenly they saw scores of people stampeding towards them in blind panic.

Shot after shot rang out.

The lawmen ran to a corner close to

a hardware store. The side wall of the building jutted out a few feet from the rest of the storefronts. It gave both lawmen cover as they searched for a hint of where the firing was coming from. Red-hot tapers cut down through the night air from the top of one of the buildings a couple of hundred yards away from them as Ben Parker began to earn his blood money.

'Them Bar Q boys must have locked horns with some of them gold miners, Marshal Fallen,' Elmer said as he checked his scattergun.

'Ya wrong.' Fallen shook his head and pointed towards the Silver Fox saloon. 'That couldn't be either the miners or the cowpunchers, Elmer. Those shots are coming from up there.'

Elmer squinted. 'Damn it all. Ya right. There's some *hombre* up there with a Winchester.'

As the lawmen ran from cover towards the corner of the Golden Garter, Parker's bullets rained down on them. The sand cut up in frozen plumes all around their boots but both men continued on to the saloon's side wall.

Then they saw the tall Appaloosa emerge from the crowd of running men and women as its inexperienced rider vainly tried to control the powerful animal.

Elmer raised both his eyebrows in surprise.

'Glory be, Marshal Fallen. Ain't that little Angie? What in tarnation is she doing on a big horse like that?'

'It sure is her, and she's in trouble.' Fallen ran out into the street towards the tiny female perched precariously on the high Mexican saddle. It was obvious to the marshal that Angie had no idea how to control any horse, least of all a great stallion like the one now cantering straight at him.

Ignoring the danger, Fallen raced through the crowd and stood in the path of the approaching Appaloosa. He waved his arms and saw the horse ease its pace. At the last possible moment he jumped at the Appaloosa's head and wrestled with its harness until the animal came to a halt.

He reached out with his muscular arms and caught the tiny Angie just as she fell from the saddle. She was like a child in the arms of the six-foot-six-inch-tall lawman. As more and more people and loose horses ran past him, Fallen carried her to the relative safety of the boardwalk and set her down next to the open-mouthed Elmer.

'Are ya OK, Angie?' Fallen asked her as another volley of lethal rifle shots tore through the air and cut down another handful of men.

'Marshal Fallen,' Angie stammered in fright.

Fallen shielded her with his body against a wall. 'Ya safe now.'

Bullets tore the wall beside them apart. A cloud of smouldering splinters showered over them.

'Ya don't understand, Marshal,' Angie pleaded.

Elmer raised his shotgun and blasted both barrels up at the high roof of the saloon. 'Whoever that is he sure has himself a lot of ammunition, Marshal Fallen.'

'Did ya get him, Elmer?' Fallen asked.

Before the deputy could answer, more venomous shots rained down on the crowd. More men spun on their heels and fell to the ground.

Elmer pulled two more cartridges from his pocket and pushed them into the smoking chambers of his shotgun. 'I ain't sure I got me the range with this old scattergun. We need us rifles like the one he's using.'

Fallen narrowed his eyes and looked across at the Appaloosa stallion, which was standing in the middle of the street amid a dozen wounded and dead men. The marshal could see the array of rifles attached to its saddle.

'Keep firing up at him.'

'But I ain't got the range, Marshal Fallen.'

'It don't matter,' Fallen insisted. 'Just make him keep his head down for a few seconds. I'll get us rifles. Cover me.'

Elmer blasted up at Ben Parker

again. As the buckshot plume filled the air the marshal raced across the sand towards the Appaloosa stallion. When he reached the animal he hauled two rifles from its saddle. Then he ran back to where the deputy and the young female were standing against a wall. He threw one rifle to Elmer, then cranked the other in his powerful hands.

Angie grabbed the marshal's collar. Fallen looked down into Angie's eyes.

'Listen to me, Marshal.'

As another barrage of rifle shots cut down into Front Street the tall lawman leaned closer to the tiny female. 'What is it? What are ya trying to say?'

'That's my pa up there doing the shooting,' Angie said, drawing him closer. 'That ain't the worst of it.'

'Then what is?' Matt Fallen asked.

'There's a varmint named Waco Walt who's been paid to kill ya, Marshal. My pa is trying to draw ya out into the open so Waco can kill ya.'

Fallen gave a slow nod of his head. 'Thanks.'

She released her grip. 'A friend of mine is trying to stop Waco before he gets ya in his sights, Marshal.'

'Who would that be, Angie?'

'His name's Jim Fury,' she replied.

'Kid Fury?'

'That's what some folks call him.'

Matt Fallen sighed heavily. 'I'm gonna have to kill ya pa, Angie. He's already shot more folks than I can count.'

She nodded sadly. 'I know.'

Matt Fallen looked at Elmer. 'Are ya ready, Elmer?'

The deputy sighed. 'Yep.'

Both lawman moved out into the moonlight and fired their rifles in quick succession. They saw the Winchester fly from Parker's hands up into the moon-light. Then they watched as the man toppled off the high roof. Parker fell straight down and crashed through a porch overhang before slamming on to the unforgiving saloon boardwalk.

'We got the sidewinder, Marshal Fallen.'

'Go check that he's dead, Elmer,' Matt Fallen said in a low drawl. He watched as his deputy raced up the street towards the body. Then he turned.

He had felt the eyes of the gunfighter watching him. Then he saw the thin, tall figure half-hidden by shadow between two buildings to his left. Suddenly a shot rang out and Fallen felt the Winchester being torn from his grip. The sheer force of the bullet crashing into the rifle sent the marshal spinning on his heels. He fell to his knees just as Waco Walt stepped away from the alley with his guns drawn.

There was a hideous smile carved in the strange features of the hired killer. Fallen could see the smoke trailing from the barrel of the gun in Waco Walt's right hand and knew that he had no chance of drawing his own six-shooter before the gunfighter squeezed his triggers again.

'How much are ya being paid to kill me, Waco?' Fallen shouted defiantly. 'And who hired ya?'

The gunfighter smiled. 'You'll never know.'

163

Matt Fallen shook his head. 'Reckon not.'

'Say ya prayers, Marshal,' Waco snarled as his long legs closed the distance between them.

The marshal lowered his head and awaited his fate.

Finale

The two men stared through the gunsmoke at one another over the countless bodies strewn across the wide street. Waco Walt stopped when he was within twenty feet of his target and pulled both his gun hammers back. He was grinning and nodding with satisfaction at the helpless marshal kneeling before him.

'Do ya reckon ya can draw that gun before I send ya to the happy hunting ground, Fallen?' Waco Walt taunted. 'Have ya got the guts to try?'

Matt Fallen gritted his teeth. He had never seen a face quite like that of Waco Walt's. The eyes hidden by fleshy hoods seemed little more than gashes but he knew they were fixed upon his every movement.

'I reckon I better try.' Fallen raised his right hand and flexed his fingers over the gun grip.

'Then try.'

Suddenly a figure walked out from an alley just behind the lawman and approached the deadly gunfighter. Kid Fury had his hands hovering just above his holstered guns. He was moving at a fearless pace towards Waco Walt. As he reached the kneeling marshal the Kid paused.

'Stay kneeling, Marshal,' Fury advised. 'Ya a mighty big target when ya standing up on them hind legs.'

Waco Walt glared furiously at the short youngster.

'Kid Fury.' The smile vanished from Waco Walt's face. His hooded eyes burned into the defiant youngster. 'I thought we left ya hogtied back at the hotel.'

'Ya did.'

The ruthless killer raised both his cocked guns and trained them on the Kid. 'Never figured that Kid Fury was suicidal.'

'I ain't,' Fury said. 'I'm gonna draw

my six-shooters and kill ya before ya can squeeze them triggers, Waco.'

'Big words for a little man. If ya recall, ya failed once before, Kid,' Waco reminded the younger man. 'I don't think that ya could have gotten any faster with them hoglegs.'

Kid Fury smiled.

Suddenly, as he saw the hands of the gunfighter move, the Kid drew one of his guns and fanned its hammer three times in quick succession. Red-hot flashes of deafening venom cut across the distance between the two men.

Choking smoke filled the street as the youngster remained beside the lawman.

Matt Fallen got to his feet. His narrowed eyes stared into the gunsmoke until the night breeze blew it away. Waco Walt was standing like a statue but his guns had dropped from his thin hands. His shirt front was stained with crimson gore. There was a confused expression on his face as he blinked hard and looked down at the trio of bullet holes in his chest. He looked at the youngster.

'Ya did get faster, Kid.'

Fury shook his head. 'No, Waco. You got slower.'

Waco Walt Dando made as though to step forward. His long legs buckled beneath him and he fell heavily into the frosty ground. A sickening, rattlesnake sound came from the gunfighter's throat as death claimed yet another victim.

Matt Fallen looked down at Kid Fury.

'Thanks, Kid,' the marshal said. 'Ya saved my bacon.'

The barefoot Angie rushed to Fury's side and wrapped her arms around him. She then looked up at the marshal, towering over both of them.

'His name's Jim, Marshal.'

The tall lawman nodded. 'So it is. My mistake.'

Fury holstered his guns as Elmer came running up to them and turned the body of Waco Walt over. As he did so a thick wad of paper money fell on to the frosty ground. The deputy plucked it up, walked to Fallon and handed it to him.

'What ya figure that varmint was doing with so much money, Marshal Fallen?' Elmer innocently asked.

'Ain't it obvious?' Matt Fallen said. 'He was keeping it for our two young friends here, Elmer.'

Elmer scratched his head. He could not hide his confusion.

Matt Fallen turned and handed the money to the two youngsters. They stared at the small fortune with eyes even more confused than those of the deputy.

'What's this for?' Fury asked.

'It ain't ours,' Angie said.

Matt Fallen smiled. 'Sure it is. It's the reward money for saving my life, children. Besides, you'll need every penny of it to fix up the hotel after ya get hitched.'

Both Fury and Angie blushed in a way that only those in love ever blush.

The youngsters walked away. Their arms were wrapped around one another as if afraid to ever let go. The marshal envied their innocence.

'Hold on a minute.' Elmer scratched his head again. 'Was that Kid Fury with Angie, Marshal Fallen?'

Matt Fallen rested a hand on the shoulder of his deputy.

'Hell, no. Didn't ya hear little Angie, Elmer? His name's Jim.'

THE END

We do hope that you have enjoyed reading this large print book.

Did you know that all of our titles are available for purchase?

We publish a wide range of high quality large print books including:
Romances, Mysteries, Classics
General Fiction
Non Fiction and Westerns

Special interest titles available in large print are:
The Little Oxford Dictionary
Music Book, Song Book
Hymn Book, Service Book

Also available from us courtesy of Oxford University Press:
Young Readers' Dictionary
(large print edition)
Young Readers' Thesaurus
(large print edition)

For further information or a free brochure, please contact us at:
Ulverscroft Large Print Books Ltd.,
The Green, Bradgate Road, Anstey,
Leicester, LE7 7FU, England.
Tel: (00 44) **0116 236 4325**
Fax: (00 44) **0116 234 0205**

Other titles in the
Linford Western Library:

SHOOTOUT AT CLEARWATER SPRINGS

Aaron Adams

River Bow Ranch is in big trouble: owing money to the bank, and with only a small, sickly herd. It looks as if Mark Merkel will be forced to hand over his business to his ruthless neighbour, Connor MacPherson, who has been eyeing the River Bow for some time. But Mark's son David refuses to be defeated, and has an audacious plan to save the ranch. Faced with an implacable enemy, and with a murderer in their midst, can the Merkels succeed?

SKELETON HAND

C. J. Sommers

Three cowboys, cut loose from the Domino ranch, head south to seek work elsewhere. Caught in a storm, they take shelter in an abandoned trapper's cabin, where they make two startling discoveries — a hoard of gold squirreled away, and a skeleton holding a hand of cards. Taking the cash, they journey on — but find themselves drawn into a lethal game with a band of killers. It seems the skeleton isn't holding the only deadly hand . . .

A MAN CALLED DRIFTER

Steve Hayes

Ingrid Bjorkman had been kid-napped. But was she just the bait in a trap meant to snare her would-be rescuers? In their long, gunsmoke-filled lives, three men — Gabriel Moonlight, Latigo Rawlins, and the man known only as Drifter — had made more than their fair share of enemies. And when the trio took to the trail, they had two more shooters to back their play: Raven, daughter of Ingrid — and Deputy US Marshal Liberty Mercer, daughter of Drifter . . .

THE DEVIL'S MARSHAL

I. J. Parnham

When Lucinda Latimer is accused of murdering Archibald Harper, her bounty hunter brother Brodie is convinced of her innocence. Vowing to find the culprit, he turns up a witness in the form of drunken varmint Wilfred Clay — who, minutes after admitting to seeing the real killer, is shot to death on his own front porch. All the clues point to the murderer being Derrick Shelby — the man known as 'the devil's marshal'. The only trouble is, Derrick died a year ago . . .

JOURNEY INTO JEOPARDY

Mark Bannerman

Former Pinkerton detective Frank Glengarry is called out of retirement to take on one final task: the delivery of a ransom to the kidnappers of Lucille Glassner, daughter of a US senator. Though assured there will be no danger, Glengarry is travelling to one of the remotest corners of California — and is about to fall foul of the law. Forced onto a trail littered with lynchings, greed, vengeance, murder and double-dealing, his only means of escape is to face up to those who want him dead . . .